The Warmth of Summer

A collection of impressions reflecting on the rich season of warmth and sunshine when spirits soar like the temperatures.

ACKNOWLEDGMENTS

Excerpts by Henry Beston: "I can watch a fine surf..." and "The three elemental sounds..." From THE OUTERMOST HOUSE by Henry Beston. Copyright 1928, 1949, © 1956 by Henry Beston. Copyright © 1977 Elizabeth C. Beston. Reprinted by permission of Holt, Rinehart and Winston, Publishers. Excerpts from the following works of John Burroughs: BIRDS AND POETS; FAR AND NEAR; LEAF AND TENDRIL; LOCUSTS AND WILD HONEY; PEPACTON; RIVERBY; SIGNS AND SEASONS; THE SUMMIT OF THE YEARS; UNDER THE MAPLES; WAKE-ROBIN; WINTER SUNSHINE. All used through courtesy of Houghton Mifflin Company, Publishers. CAMPING by Larry Roger Clark. From SPEAK TO THE EARTH by Larry Roger Clark. Copyright © 1972 by Larry Roger Clark. Published by Dorrance & Company. Excerpts by Wallace Kirkland: "Sweet clover, unlike spiderwort..."; "The first mosquito of the night..."; "Mosquitoes multiply rapidly..."; "The early morning was set aside ..." Reprinted from THE LURE OF THE POND by Wallace Kirkland, Copyright © 1969 with the permission of Contemporary Books, Inc., Chicago. Excerpt by Joseph Wood Krutch: "This is the very dead... confident weeds." from THE BEST NATURE WRITING OF JOSEPH WOOD KRUTCH (1970) Copyright 1949 by Joseph Wood Krutch. By permission of William Morrow & Company. Specified 8 excerpts by Sigurd F. Olson: "I never watch a sunset..."; "Beauty is composed of many things..."; "I have had my share of solitude..."; "Everyone needs such quiet times..."; "On a trip long ago..."; "It is not surprising..."; "In the wilderness..."; "I noticed this phenomenon..." From REFLECTIONS FROM THE NORTH COUNTRY, by Sigurd F. Olson. Copyright © 1976 by Sigurd F. Olson. Reprinted by permission of Alfred A. Knopf, Inc. Specified excerpts by Sigurd F. Olson from pages 84-85 and 86-87 from "Moon Magic": "When the moon shines..."; "If humans in all their sophistication..." From THE SINGING WILDERNESS, by Sigurd F. Olson. Copyright © 1956 by Sigurd F. Olson. Reprinted by permission of Alfred A. Knopf, Inc. Specified 11 excerpts by Sigurd F. Olson: "The movement of a canoe ..."; "For countless thousands of years..."; "To recapture the spirit..."; "Something happens to a man..."; "Rapids, too, are a challenge..."; "The canoe gives a sense of..."; "It is as free as the wind itself..."; "There is a magic..."; "That day, with white horses..."; "Once a man has known..."; "There have been countless campfires..." From SIGURD F. OLSON'S WILDERNESS DAYS, by Sigurd F. Olson. Copyright © 1956, 1958, 1961, 1963, 1969, 1972 by Sigurd F. Olson. Reprinted by permission of Alfred A. Knopf, Inc. THE CIRCUS-DAY PARADE and KNEE-DEEP IN JUNE by James Whitcomb Riley. From THE BIOGRAPHICAL EDITION OF THE COMPLETE WORKS OF JAMES WHITCOMB RILEY by The Bobbs-Merrill Company, Inc., Publishers. THE HARVEST of Clara B. Dice Roe. From THE SINGING PRAIRIE by Clara B. Dice Roe. Copyright © 1960 by Dorrance & Company. QUEEN'S LACE by Edith H. Shank. From THE KEY RING by Edith H. Shank. Copyright © 1958 by Dorrance & Company. EVENSONG by Robert Louis Stevenson. From SONGS OF TRAVEL by Robert Louis Stevenson. (Charles Scribner's Sons). Excerpts by Edwin Way Teale: "Between these two events..."; "Half a mile or so downstream..."; "There are more than forty orders..."; "Around the world..."; "None of the scenes..."; "In nature the shades of green..."; "A spectacular feature ..."; "One stalk of corn ..." Reprinted by permission of DODD, MEAD & COMPANY, INC. from JOURNEY INTO SUMMER by Edwin Way Teale. Copyright © 1960 by Edwin Way Teale. Excerpts by Edwin Way Teale: "On this hot and humid day..."; "When July Comes..." Reprinted by permission of DODD, MEAD & COMPANY, INC. from A WALK THROUGH THE YEAR by Edwin Way Teale. Copyright © 1978 by Edwin Way Teale. All Henry David Thoreau material used through courtesy of Houghton Mifflin Company, Publishers. Our sincere thanks to the following author whose address we were unable to locate: E. F. Hayward for BACK TO NATURE.

PHOTO CREDITS

Larry Backe, 1; Robert Campbell, 22; Circus World Museum—Baraboo, Wisconsin, 58; Ed Cooper, 13, 14, 17, 18, 20, 24, 25, 30, 38; Fred Dole, 68; John Ebeling, 36; Freelance Photographers Guild, 80; Grant Heilman, 27, 34, 46, 66, 70, 72; Lick Observatory—University of California, 10; Milwaukee Public Museum, 49, 50, 52 (2), 54, 56 (2), 60 (top), 74 (2), 78; National Oceanic and Atmospheric Administration (Allan Moller), 6; National Park Service, 31, 40; Ted Schiffman, 65 (top); Tom Stack and Associates, cover, 4, 8, 12, 28, 45, 48; John Strang, 60 (bottom); United States Department of Agriculture, 16, 44 (2), 65 (bottom), 76 (2); Wisconsin Department of Natural Resources, 33.

Editorial Director, James Kuse

Managing Editor, Ralph Luedtke

Production Editor/Manager, Richard Lawson

Photographic Editor, Gerald Koser

Copy Editor, Sharon Style

designed and edited by

David Schansberg

How welcome the warmth, too! We had stepped from April into June, with the mercury near the seventies, and our spirits rose accordingly.

John Burroughs

Between these two events in time and space stretches the season of warmth and sunshine. Summer is vacation time, sweet clover time, swing and see-saw time, watermelon time, swimming and picnic and camping and Fourth-of-July time. This is the season of gardens and flowers, of haying and threshing. Summer is the period when birds have fewer feathers and furbearers have fewer hairs in their pelts. Through it runs the singing of insects, the sweetness of ripened fruit, the perfume of unnumbered blooms. It is a time of lambs and colts, kittens and puppies, a time to grow in. It is fishing time, canoeing time, baseball time. It is for millions of Americans, "The good old summertime."

Edwin Way Teale

Summer

Summer begins in June. It comes after the wild excitement of spring, the migration of birds, their mating and choosing of places to live and defend. It is a time of fullness and completion, the goal of all that has gone before, a time of feeding the young on the clouds of insects, on the hosts of worms and grubs in the fertile humus and new fruits with which the earth is now blessed. All living creatures gorge themselves and their young on the food that is at this season so rich and abundant. It is a time for building strength and storing energy for whatever may come. It is also a time of joy.

In the warmth of rains and sunny days, the forest floor literally teems with life. Seeds swell and burst and grow, colored fungi and lichens all but spring from the ground. Flowers are bolder in their hues than those of spring. They bloom in crannies on cliffs, on bare rock faces, in swamps and forest shades. Dwarf dogwood stipples the ground, drifts of pink linnaea lie beneath the pines, while cherries and plums lace woodland borders in fantastic designs. There is a sense of almost tropical lushness after the stark severities of winter.

Because there is so much of everything, there is a relaxation in effort and even time for playing in the sun. In the mornings the mists roll out of the bays, pink when the days are bright, ghostly white when they are dark. In the evenings the loons call, while hermit thrushes and whitethroats warble in the aspen.

This is the essence of summer—a time of plenty and a soft green beauty in which hardships, survival, and eternal striving belong to a different and almost forgotten time.

Sigurd F. Olson

3

Warm, mellow summer. The glowing sunbeams make every nerve tingle.

John Muir

As you read a man's purpose in his face, so you learn to read the purpose of the weather in the face of the day.

John Burroughs

Let me have a draught of undiluted morning air. Morning air! If men will not drink of this at the fountainhead of the day, why, then, we must even bottle up some and sell it in the shops, for the benefit of those who have lost their subscription ticket to morning time in this world. But remember, it will not keep quite till noonday even in the coolest cellar, but drive out the stopples long ere that and follow westward the steps of Aurora.

Henry David Thoreau

The critical moments of the day as regards the weather are at sunrise and sunset. A clear sunset is always a good sign; an obscured sun, just at the moment of going down after a bright day, bodes storm. There is much truth, too, in the saying that if it rain before seven, it will clear before eleven. Nine times in ten it will turn out thus.

John Burroughs

Summer begins now, about a week past, with the expanded leaves, the shade, and warm weather. Cultivated fields, too, are leaving out, that is, corn and potatoes coming up. Most trees are leaved and are now forming fruit. Young berries, too, are forming, and birds are being hatched. . . . It is now the season of growth.

Henry David Thoreau

Nearly every season I note what I call the bridal day of summer—a white, lucid, shining day, with a delicate veil of mist softening all outlines. How the river dances and sparkles; how the new leaves of all the trees shine under the sun; the air has a soft lustre; there is a haze, it is not blue, but a kind of shining, diffused nimbus. No clouds, the sky a bluish white, very soft and delicate. It is the nuptial day of the season; the sun fairly takes the earth to be his own, for better or for worse, on such a day, and what marriages there are going on all about us: the marriages of the flowers, of the bees, of the birds. Everything suggests life, love, fruition. These bridal days are often repeated; the serenity and equipoise of the elements combine. . . .

John Burroughs

Summer Wind

It is a sultry day; the sun has drunk
The dew that lay upon the morning grass;
There is no rustling in the lofty elm
That canopies my dwelling, and its shade
Scarce cools me. All is silent, save the faint
And interrupted murmur of the bee,
Settling on the sick flowers, and then again
Instantly on the wing. The plants around
Feel the too potent fervors: the tall maize
Rolls up its long green leaves; the clover droops
Its tender foliage, and declines its blooms.
But far in the fierce sunshine tower the hills,
With all their growth of woods, silent and stern,
As if the scorching heat and dazzling light
Were but an element they loved. Bright clouds,
Motionless pillars of the brazen heaven—
Their bases on the mountains—their white tops
Shining in the far ether—fire the air
With a reflected radiance, and make turn
The gazer's eye away. For me, I lie
Languidly in the shade, where the thick turf,
Yet virgin from the kisses of the sun,
Retains some freshness, and I woo the wind
That still delays his coming. Why so slow,
Gentle and voluble spirit of the air?
Oh, come and breathe upon the fainting earth
Coolness and life. Is it that in his caves
He hears me? See, on yonder woody ridge,
The pine is bending his proud top, and now
Among the nearer groves, chestnut and oak
Are tossing their green boughs about. He comes;
Lo, where the grassy meadow runs in waves!
The deep distressful silence of the scene
Breaks up with mingling of unnumbered sounds
And universal motion. He is come,
Shaking a shower of blossoms from the shrubs,
And bearing on their fragrance; and he brings
Music of birds, and rustling of young boughs,
And sound of swaying branches, and the voice
Of distant waterfalls. All the green herbs
Are stirring in his breath; a thousand flowers,
By the roadside and the borders of the brook,
Nod gayly to each other; glossy leaves
Are twinkling in the sun, as if the dew
Were on them yet, and silver waters break
Into small waves and sparkle as he comes.

William Cullen Bryant

Warm, sunny day, thrilling plant and animals and rocks alike, making sap and blood flow fast, and making every particle of the crystal mountains throb and swirl and dance in glad accord like star dust. No dullness anywhere visible or thinkable. No stagnation, no death. Everything kept in joyful rhythmic motion in the pulses of nature's big heart.

John Muir

The summer days are come again;
Once more the glad earth yields
Her golden wealth of ripening grain,
And breath of clover fields,
And deepening shade of summer woods,
And glow of summer air,
And winging thoughts, and happy moods
Of love and joy and prayer.

The summer days are come again;
The birds are on the wing;
God's praises, in their loving strain,
Unconsciously they sing.
We know who giveth all the good
That doth our cup o'erbrim . . .
For summer joy in field and wood
We lift our song to Him.

Samuel Longfellow

Rain in Summer

How beautiful is the rain!
After the dust and heat,
In the broad and fiery street,
In the narrow lane,
How beautiful is the rain!

How it clatters along the roofs,
Like the tramp of hoofs!
How it gushes and struggles out
From the throat of the overflowing spout!
Across the windowpane
It pours and pours;
And swift and wide,
With a muddy tide,
Like a river down the gutter roars
The rain, the welcome rain!

The sick man from his chamber looks
At the twisted brooks;
He can feel the cool
Breath of each little pool;
His fevered brain
Grows calm again,
And he breathes a blessing on the rain.

From the neighboring school
Come the boys,
With more than their wonted noise
And commotion;
And down the wet streets
Sail their mimic fleets,
Till the treacherous pool
Engulfs them in its whirling
And turbulent ocean.

In the country, on every side,
Where far and wide,
Like a leopard's tawny and spotted hide,

Stretches the plain,
To the dry grass and the drier grain
How welcome is the rain!

In the furrowed land
The toilsome and patient oxen stand;
Lifting the yoke-encumbered head,
With their dilated nostrils spread,
They silently inhale
The clover-scented gale,
And the vapors that arise
From the well-watered and smoking soil.
For this rest in the furrow after toil
Their large and lustrous eyes
Seem to thank the Lord,
More than man's spoken word.

Near at hand,
From under the sheltering trees,
The farmer sees
His pastures, and his fields of grain,
As they bend their tops
To the numberless beating drops
Of the incessant rain.
He counts it as no sin
That he sees therein
Only his own thrift and gain.

These, and far more than these,
The Poet sees!
He can behold
Aquarius old
Walking the fenceless fields of air;
And from each ample fold
Of the clouds about him rolled
Scattering everywhere
The showery rain,
As the farmer scatters his grain.

Henry Wadsworth Longfellow

But the great fact about the rain is that it is the most beneficent of all the operations of nature; more immediately than sunlight even, it means life and growth. Moisture is the Eve of the physical world, the soft teeming principle given to wife to Adam or heat, and the mother of all that lives. Sunshine abounds everywhere, but only where the rain or dew follows is there life.

I suppose there is some compensation in a drought; nature doubtless profits by it in some way. It is a good time to thin out her garden and give the law of the survival of the fittest a chance to come into play. How the big trees and big plants do rob the little ones! there is not drink enough to go around, and the strongest will have what there is. It is a rest to vegetation, too, a kind of torrid winter that is followed by a fresh awakening. Every tree and plant learns a lesson from it, learns to shoot its roots down deep into the perennial supplies of moisture and life.

But when the rain does come, the warm, sun-distilled rain; the far-traveling, vapor-born rain; the impartial, undiscriminating, unstinted rain; equable, bounteous, myriad eyed, searching out every plant and every spear of grass, finding every hidden thing that needs water, falling upon the just and upon the unjust, sponging off every leaf of every tree in the forest and every growth in the fields; music to the ear, a perfume to the smell, an enchantment to the eye; healing the earth, cleansing the air, renewing the fountains; honey to the

Around the world, night and day, it is estimated that there are about 1,800 thunderstorms in progress at any given time. On the same world-wide basis, there are about 100 flashes of lightning every second of the year.

Edwin Way Teale

bee, manna to the herds, and life to all creatures —what spectacle so fills the heart?

John Burroughs

It is worth the while to have had a cloudy, even a stormy, day for an excursion, if only that you are out at the clearing up. The beauty of the landscape is greater, not only by reason of the contrast with its recent lowering aspect, but because of the greater freshness and purity of the air and of vegetation, and of the repressed and so recruited spirits of the beholder. Sunshine is nothing to be observed or described but when it is seen in patches on the hillsides, or suddenly bursts forth with splendor at the end of a storm. I derive pleasure now from the shadows of the clouds diversifying the sunshine on the hills, where lately all was shadow. The spirits of the cows at pasture on this very hillside appear excited. They are restless from a kind of joy, and are not content with feeding. The weedy shore is suddenly blotted out by this rise of waters.

Henry David Thoreau

In flashes, less than a ten-thousandth of a second in duration, lightning ripped through the dark clouds on either hand. One thunderbolt ran zigzag along the horizon to our right. Each stroke hurled the vast explosion of its thunder over us. Yet we seemed less in the midst of the storm than running between two storms. Steadily the darkest clouds, the brightest flashes, the loudest cannonading moved away behind us. We were through the arch and under lighter sky. Then the deluge began.

Edwin Way Teale

After the Storm

How glorious to see the sun
After the storm is o'er.
The storm clouds roll back as a scroll,
The earth is bright once more.

And so it is in each our lives . . .
Sometimes the darkness falls,
Sometimes we wander aimlessly,
The waves mount up as walls.

But soon the blue comes peeking through,
The troubles pass away
And we are left, richer by far
For troubles have a way

Of teaching lessons to us all.
Let's bow our heads before
The God who brings the inner calm
After the storm is o'er.

Georgia B. Adams

It is fixed there against the cloud, irrespective of the falling motion of the drops of rain through which it is formed. They fall, but it does not fall. They are swayed or whirled by the wind, but the bow keeps its place. That band of prismatic colors is in no sense a part of the rain, and the rain knows it not. It springs out in the rear of the retreating storm, but the storm knows it not. The eye knows it not, and sees it not unless placed at a certain definite point in relation to it. The point of view makes the bow. No two persons see precisely the same rainbow; there are as many bows as there are beholders.

Sometimes we see two rainbows, as if nature were in an extra happy mood. In the second one the colors are in reverse order from that of the first. The first is due to the rays of the sun falling upon the outer portions of the drops and suffering two refractions and one reflec-

Whose heart does not leap up, be he child or man, when he beholds a rainbow in the sky? It is the most spectacular as it is the most beautiful thing in the familiar daily nature about us. It has all the qualities that are most calculated to surprise and delight us—suddenness, brilliancy, delicacy, sharp contrasts, and the primal cosmic form, the circle.

John Burroughs

tion before reaching the eye, while the second bow is due to the rays falling on the inner side of the drops and suffering two refractions and two reflections.

The rainbow is an apparition of color and form in the air. It is not so much an entity as the radiant shadow of an entity—fugitive, unreal, phantasmal, unapproachable, yet as constant as the sun and rain.

The sunset is afar off, painted upon the distant clouds, but the rainbow comes down to earth and spans the next field or valley. It hovers about the playing fountain; it beams out from the swaying spray of the cataract. It is as familiar as the day, yet as elusive as a spirit—a bow of promise, indeed—a symbol of the peace, the moderation, and the beneficence in nature that brought man upon the earth and now sustains him here.

John Burroughs

My Heart Leaps Up

My heart leaps up when I behold
  A rainbow in the sky:
So was it when my life began,
So is it now I am a man,
So be it when I shall grow old
  Or let me die!
The child is father of the man:
And I could wish my days to be
Bound each to each by natural piety.

William Wordsworth

The rain brought out the colors of the woods with delightful freshness, the rich brown of the bark of the trees and the fallen burs and leaves and dead ferns; the grays of rocks and lichens; the light purple of swelling buds, and the warm yellow greens of the libocedrus and mosses. The air was steaming with delightful fragrance, not rising and wafting past in separate masses, but diffused through all the atmosphere. Pine woods are always fragrant, but most so in spring when the young tassels are opening and in warm weather when the various gums and balsams are softened by the sun. The wind was now chafing their innumerable needles and the warm rain was steeping them. Monardella grows here in large beds in the openings, and there is plenty of laurel in dells and manzanita on the hillsides, and the rosy, fragrant chamoebatia carpets the ground almost everywhere. These, with the gums and balsams of the woods, form the main local fragrance-fountains of the storm.

John Muir

Another midday cloudland, displaying power and beauty that one never wearies in beholding, but hopelessly unsketchable and untellable. What can poor mortals say about clouds? While a description of their huge glowing domes and ridges, shadowy gulfs and canyons, and feather-edged ravines is being tried, they vanish, leaving no visible ruins. . . .

John Muir

9

> *The man who has seen the rising moon break out of the clouds at midnight has been present like an archangel at the creation of light and of the world.*
>
> Ralph Waldo Emerson

I went to bed early last night, but found myself waked shortly after 12, and, turning awhile sleepless and mentally feverish, I rose, dressed myself, sallied forth, and walked down the lane. The full moon, some three or four hours up—a sprinkle of light and less-light clouds just lazily moving—Jupiter an hour high in the east, and here and there throughout the heavens a random star appearing and disappearing. So, beautifully veiled and varied— the air, with that early-summer perfume, not at all damp or raw—at times Luna languidly emerging in richest brightness for minutes, and then partially enveloped again. Far off a whippoorwill plied his notes incessantly. It was that silent time between 1 and 3. The rare nocturnal scene, how soon it soothed and pacified me! Is there not something about the moon, some relation or reminder, which no poem or literature has yet caught?

Walt Whitman

If humans in all their sophistication permit moonlight to affect them, how much more does it affect animals? In my own moonlit wanderings I have had abundant occasion to see what it does and how animals in the wild respond to its charm. I have listened to loons go into ecstasies on wilderness lakes, have heard them call the whole night through and dash across the water as though possessed. I

spruces of the far shore. Then, as it almost reluctantly paled, we took to our paddles again. We searched and searched and found a long point from which we could see both sunset and moonrise at the same time. The calling of the loons meant more after that, and as the dusk settled all were aware of something new in their lives.

Sigurd F. Olson

When the moon shines as it did last night, I am filled with unrest and the urge to range valleys and climb mountains. I want vistas of moonlit country from high places, must see the silver of roaring rapids and sparkling lakes. At such times I must escape houses and towns and all that is confining, be a part of the moon-drenched landscape and its continental sweep. It is only when the moon is full that I feel this way, only when it rises as it did last night, round and mellow as a great orange cheese over the horizon, slow-moving and majestic.

Sigurd F. Olson

This is the most glorious part of this day, the serenest, warmest, brightest part, and the most suggestive. Evening is fairer than morning. It is chaste eve, for it has sustained the trials of the day, but to the morning such praise was inapplicable. It is incense-breathing. Morning is full of promise and vigor. Evening is pensive. The serenity is far more remarkable to those who are on the water. That part of the sky just above the horizon seen reflected, apparently, some rods off from the boat is as light a blue as the actual, but it goes on deepening as your eye draws nearer to the boat, until, when you look directly down at the reflection of the zenith, it is lost in the blackness of the water. It passes through all degrees of dark blue, and the threatening aspect of a cloud is very much enhanced in the reflection. As I wish to be on the water at sunset, I let the boat float. I enjoy now the warmth of summer with some of the water prospect of spring. Looking westward, the surface of the water on the meadows in the sun has a slight dusty appearance, with clear black lines. . . .

Henry David Thoreau

have heard sleepy birds begin to sing at midnight, wolves, foxes, frogs, and owls respond to the same inherent urge.

Sigurd F. Olson

On a trip long ago, I remember the first impact of a rising full moon. We were in the open on a great stretch of water, with islands in the far distance. The sky gradually brightened and an orange slice of moon appeared; we watched as the great sight unfolded before us. At that moment, the city men in the party caught a hint of its meaning. They were entranced as the moon became clear: pulsating as though alive, it rose slowly above the serrated

Evensong

The embers of the day are red
Beyond the murky hill.
The kitchen smokes;
The bed in the darkling
House is spread:
The great sky darkens overhead,
And the great woods are shrill.
So far have I been led,
Lord, by Thy will:
So far have I followed,
Lord, and wondered still.
The breeze from the
Embalmed land
Blows sudden towards the shore,
And claps my cottage door.
I hear the signal, Lord—
I understand.
The night at Thy command
Comes.
I will eat and sleep and
Will not question more.

Robert Louis Stevenson

I never watch a sunset without feeling the scene before me is more beautiful than any painting could possibly be, for it has the additional advantage of constant change, is never the same from one instant to the next. When one considers the sound effects that go with it in the north, the calling loons, the whisper of wings overhead, their silhouettes against the glow, the scene has such significance it is hard to leave until dark comes and the west, with the iridescence of waters, has changed to the black of night. Nothing can equal this.

Sigurd F. Olson

Now comes the sundown. The west is all a glory of color transfiguring everything. Far up the Pilot Peak Ridge the radiant host of trees stand hushed and thoughtful, receiving the sun's goodnight, as solemn and impressive a leave-taking as if sun and trees were to meet no more. The daylight fades, the color spell is broken, and the forest breathes free in the night breeze beneath the stars.

John Muir

Night is a dead monotonous period under a roof; but in the open world it passes lightly, with its stars and dews and perfumes, and the hours are marked by changes in the face of Nature. What seems a kind of temporal death to people choked between walls and curtains, is only a light and living slumber to the man who sleeps a-field. All night long he can hear Nature breathing deeply and freely; even as she takes her rest, she turns and smiles; and there is one stirring hour unknown to those who dwell in houses, when a wakeful influence goes abroad over the sleeping hemisphere, and all the outdoor world are on their feet. It is then that the cock first crows, not this time to announce the dawn, but like a cheerful watchman speeding the course of night. Cattle awake on the meadows; sheep break their fast on dewy hillsides, and change to a new lair among the ferns; and houseless men, who have lain down with the fowls, open their dim eyes and behold the beauty of the night.

Robert Louis Stevenson

The Day Is Done

The day is done, and the darkness
Falls from the wings of Night,
As a feather is wafted downward
From an eagle in his flight.

I see the lights of the village
Gleam through the rain and the mist,
And a feeling of sadness comes o'er me
That my soul cannot resist:

A feeling of sadness and longing,
That is not akin to pain,
And resembles sorrow only
As the mist resembles the rain.

Come, read to me some poem,
Some simple and heartfelt lay,
That shall soothe this restless feeling,
And banish the thoughts of day.

Not from the grand old masters,
Not from the bards sublime,
Whose distant footsteps echo
Through the corridors of Time.

For, like strains of martial music,
Their mighty thoughts suggest
Life's endless toil and endeavor;
And tonight I long for rest.

Read from some humbler poet,
Whose songs gushed from his heart
As showers from the clouds of summer,
Or tears from the eyelids start;

Who, through long days of labor,
And nights devoid of ease,
Still heard in his soul the music
Of wonderful melodies.

Such songs have power to quiet
The restless pulse of care,
And come like the benediction
That follows after prayer.

Then read from the treasured volume
The poem of thy choice,
And lend to the rhyme of the poet
The beauty of thy voice.

And the night shall be filled with music,
And the cares, that infest the day,
Shall fold their tents, like the Arabs,
And as silently steal away.

Henry Wadsworth Longfellow

The seashore is a sort of neutral ground, a most advantageous point from which to contemplate this world. It is even a trivial place. The waves forever rolling to the land are too far-travelled and untamable to be familiar....

Henry David Thoreau

Nothing about the sea is more impressive than its ceaseless rocking. John Burroughs

All the morning we had heard the sea roar on the eastern shore, which was several miles distant . . . though a schoolboy, whom we overtook, hardly knew what we meant, his ears were so used to it. He would have more plainly heard the same sound in a shell. It was a very inspiriting sound to walk by, filling the whole air, that of the sea dashing against the land, heard several miles inland. Instead of having a dog to growl before your door, to have an Atlantic Ocean to growl for a whole Cape! On the whole, we were glad of the storm, which would show us the ocean in its angriest mood.

Henry David Thoreau

The three great elemental sounds in nature are the sound of rain, the sound of wind in a primeval wood, and the sound of outer ocean on a beach. I have heard them all, and of the three elemental voices, that of ocean is the most awesome, beautiful, and varied. For it is a mistake to talk of the monotone of ocean or of the monotonous nature of its sound. The sea has many voices. Listen to the surf, really lend it your ears, and you will hear it in a world of sounds: hollow boomings and heavy roarings, great watery tumblings and tramplings, long hissing seethes, sharp, rifle-shot reports, splashes, whispers, the grinding undertone of stones, and sometimes vocal sounds that might be the half-heard talk of people of the sea.

Henry Beston

When one first catches the smell of the sea, his lungs seem involuntarily to expand, the same as they do when he steps into the open air after long confinement indoors. On the beach he is simply emerging into a larger and more primitive out-of-doors. There before him is aboriginal space, and the breath of it thrills and dilates his body. He stands at the open door of the continent and eagerly drinks the large air. This breeze savors of the original element; it is a breath out of the morning of the world—bitter, but so fresh and tonic! He has

I can watch a fine surf for hours, taking pleasure in all its wild plays and variations. I like to stand on my beach, watching a long wave start breaking in many places, and see the curling water run north and south from the several beginnings, and collide in furious white pyramids built of the opposing energies. Splendid fountains often delight the eye. . . .

Henry Beston

taken salt grossly and at secondhand all his days; now let him inhale it at the fountainhead, and let its impalpable crystals penetrate his spirit and prick and chafe him into new activity.

John Burroughs

Sometimes the waves look like revolving cylindrical knives, carving the coast. Then they thrust up their thin, crescent-shaped edges, like reapers, reaping only shells and sand; yet one seems to hear the hiss of a great sickle, the crackle of stubble, the rustle of sheaves, and the screening of grain. Then again there is mimic thunder as the waves burst, followed by a sound like the downpouring of torrents of rain. How it shovels the sand and sifts and washes it forever! Every particle of silt goes seaward; it is the earth pollen with which the sunken floors of the sea are deeply covered. . . .

John Burroughs

The Tide Rises, The Tide Falls

The tide rises, the tide falls,
The twilight darkens, the curlew calls;
Along the sea sands damp and brown
The traveller hastens toward the town,
And the tide rises, the tide falls.

Darkness settles on roofs and walls,
But the sea, the sea in the darkness calls;
The little waves, with their soft, white hands,
Efface the footprints in the sands,
And the tide rises, the tide falls.

The morning breaks; the steeds in their stalls
Stamp and neigh, as the hostler calls;
The day returns, but nevermore
Returns the traveller to the shore,
And the tide rises, the tide falls.

Henry Wadsworth Longfellow

The sea awoke at midnight from its sleep,
And round the pebbly beaches far and wide
I heard the first wave of the rising tide
Rush onward with uninterrupted sweep;

A voice out of the silence of the deep,
A sound mysteriously multiplied
As of a cataract from the mountain's side,
Or roar of winds upon a wooded steep.

So comes to us at times, from the unknown
And inaccessible solitudes of being,
The rushing of the sea-tides of the soul;

And inspirations, that we deem our own,
Are some divine foreshadowing and foreseeing
Of things beyond our reason or control.

Henry Wadsworth Longfellow

The Sound of the Sea

I saw the long line of the vacant shore,
The seaweed and the shells upon the sand,
And the brown rocks left bare on every hand,
As if the ebbing tide would flow no more.

Then heard I, more distinctly than before,
The ocean breathe and its great breast expand,
And hurrying came on the defenceless land
The insurgent waters with tumultuous roar.

All thought and feeling and desire, I said,
Love, laughter, and the exultant joy of song
Have ebbed from me forever! Suddenly o'er me

They swept again from their deep ocean bed,
And in a tumult of delight, and strong
As youth, and beautiful as youth, upbore me.

Henry Wadsworth Longfellow

15

> *Nature never appears more serene and innocent and fragrant. A hundred white lilies, open to the sun, rest on the surface smooth as oil amid their pads, while devil's-needles are glancing over them.*
>
> Henry David Thoreau

A field of water betrays the spirit that is in the air. It is continually receiving new life and motion from above. It is intermediate in its nature between land and sky. On land only the grass and trees wave, but the water itself is rippled by the wind. I see where the breeze dashes across it by the streaks or flakes of light. It is remarkable that we can look down on its surface.

Henry David Thoreau

A Lake in Summer

A lake in the summer,
Like the whole wide world
Without man-made complexities,
Has all the things that make life good.

A lake can hold blue sky,
Gold sun, bright stars, the moon;
Lined clouds, white birds, tall trees,
And mountains upside down.

A summer breeze
Sends ripples of delight
Across its face.

The lake is calm,
Not rushed like man himself;
It is the world of simple things,
Not stores and cars and big machines.

It holds the key
To life itself . . .
A peacefulness inspired
By ordinary things of nature's bounds.

Nancy McCowell

Walden is a perfect forest mirror, set round with stones as precious to my eye as if fewer or rarer. Nothing so fair, so pure, and at the same time so large, as a lake, perchance, lies on the surface of the earth. Sky water. It needs no fence. Nations come and go without defiling it. It is a mirror which no stone can crack, whose quicksilver will never wear off, whose gilding Nature continually repairs; no storms, no dust, can dim its surface ever fresh—a mirror in which all impurity presented to it sinks, swept and dusted by the sun's hazy brush—this the light dustcloth—which retains no breath that is breathed on it, but sends its own to float as clouds high above its surface, and be reflected in its bosom still.

Henry David Thoreau

This small lake was of most value as a neighbor in the intervals of a gentle rainstorm in August, when, both air and water being perfectly still, but the sky overcast, mid-afternoon had all the serenity of the evening, and the wood thrush sang around, and was heard from shore to shore. A lake like this is never smoother than at such a time; and the clear portion of the air above it being shallow and darkened by clouds, the water, full of light and reflections, becomes a lower heaven itself so much the more important.

Henry David Thoreau

The wind exposes the red undersides of the white lily pads. This is one of the aspects of the river now. The bud-bearing stem of this plant is a little larger, but otherwise like the leaf-stem, and coming like it directly from the long, large root. It is interesting to pull up the lily root with flowers and leaves attached and see how it sends its buds upward to the light and air to expand and flower in another element. How interesting the bud's progress from the water to the air! So many of these stems are leaf-bearing, and so many flower-bearing. Then consider how defended these plants against drought, at the bottom of the water, at most their leaves and flowers floating on its surface. How much mud and water are required to support their vitality!

Henry David Thoreau

A lake is the landscape's most beautiful and expressive feature. It is earth's eye; looking into which the beholder measures the depth of his own nature. The fluviatile trees next the shore are the slender eyelashes which fringe it, and the wooded hills and cliffs around are its overhanging brows.

Henry David Thoreau

My Heart's in the Highlands

My heart's in the Highlands, my heart is not here;
My heart's in the Highlands a-chasing the deer;
A-chasing the wild deer, and following the roe,
My heart's in the Highlands wherever I go.

Farewell to the Highlands, farewell to the North,
The birthplace of valor, the country of worth;
Wherever I wander, wherever I rove,
The hills of the Highlands forever I love.

Farewell to the mountains high covered with snow;
Farewell to the straths and green valleys below;
Farewell to the forests and wild-hanging woods;
Farewell to the torrents and loud-pouring floods.

My heart's in the Highlands, my heart is not here;
My heart's in the Highlands a-chasing the deer,
A-chasing the wild deer, and following the roe,
My heart's in the Highlands wherever I go.

Robert Burns

My eyes had never before beheld such beauty in a mountain stream. The water was almost as transparent as the air—was, indeed, like liquid air; and as it lay in these wells and pits enveloped in shadow, or lit up by a chance ray of the vertical sun, it was a perpetual feast to the eye—so cool, so deep, so pure; every reach and pool like a vast spring. You lay down and drank or dipped the water up in your cup and found it just the right degree of refreshing coldness. One is never prepared for the clearness of the water in these streams. It is always a surprise. See them every year for a dozen years, and yet, when you first come upon one, you will utter an exclamation. . . .

John Burroughs

But the prettiest thing was the stream soliloquizing in such musical tones there amid the moss-covered rocks and boulders. How clean it looked, what purity! Civili-

I stood upon the hills, when heaven's wide arch
Was glorious with the sun's returning march,
And woods were brightened, and soft gales
Went forth to kiss the sun-clad vales.
The clouds were far beneath me; bathed in light,
They gathered midway round the wooded height,
And, in their fading glory, shone
Like hosts in battle overthrown,
As many a pinnacle, with shifting glance,
Through the gray mist thrust up its shattered lance,
And rocking on the cliff was left
The dark pine blasted, bare, and cleft.
The veil of cloud was lifted, and below
Glowed the rich valley, and the river's flow
Was darkened by the forest's shade,
Or glistened in the white cascade;
Where upward, in the mellow blush of day,
The noisy bittern wheeled his spiral way.

I heard the distant waters dash,
I saw the current whirl and flash,
And richly, by the blue lake's silver beach,
The woods were bending with a silent reach.
Then o'er the vale, with gentle swell,
The music of the village bell
Came sweetly to the echo-giving hills;
And the wild horn, whose voice the woodland fills,
Was ringing to the merry shout
That faint and far the glen sent out,
Where, answering to the sudden shot, thin smoke,
Through thick-leaved branches, from the dingle broke.

If thou art worn and hard beset
With sorrows, that thou wouldst forget,
If thou wouldst read a lesson, that will keep
Thy heart from fainting and thy soul from sleep,
Go to the woods and hills! No tears
Dim the sweet look that Nature wears.

Henry Wadsworth Longfellow

zation corrupts the streams as it corrupts the Indian; only in such remote woods can you now see a brook in all its original freshness and beauty. Only the sea and the mountain forest brook are pure; all between is contaminated more or less by the work of man. An ideal trout brook was this, now hurrying, now loitering, now deepening around a great boulder, now gliding evenly over a pavement of green-gray stone and pebbles; no sediment or stain of any kind, but white and sparkling as snow-water, and nearly as cool.

John Burroughs

All the larger streams of uncultivated countries are mysteriously charming and beautiful, whether flowing in mountains or through swamps and plains. Their channels are interestingly sculptured, far more so than the grandest architectural works of man. The finest of the forests are usually found along their banks, and in the multitude of falls and rapids in the wilderness finds a voice. Such a river is the Hiwassee, with its surface broken to a thousand sparkling gems, and its forest walls vine-draped and flowery as Eden. And how fine the songs it sings!

John Muir

A small river or stream flowing by one's door has many attractions over a large body of water like the Hudson. One can make a companion of it; he can walk with it and sit with it, or lounge on its banks, and feel that it is all his own. It becomes something private and special to him. You cannot have the same kind of attachment and sympathy with a great river; it does not flow through your affections like a lesser stream.

John Burroughs

Climb the mountains and get their good tidings. Nature's peace will flow into you as sunshine flows into trees. The winds will blow their own freshness into you, and the storms their energy, while cares will drop off like falling leaves.

John Muir

How glorious a greeting the sun gives the mountains! To behold this alone is worth the pains of any excursion a thousand times over.

John Muir

There is nothing more eloquent in nature than a mountain stream, and this is the first I ever saw. Its banks are luxuriantly peopled with rare and lovely flowers and over arching trees, making one of nature's coolest and most hospitable places.

John Muir

The finishing touch is given by the moss with which the rock is everywhere carpeted. Even in the narrow grooves or channels where the water runs the swiftest, the green lining is unbroken. It sweeps down under the stream and up again on the other side, like some firmly woven texture. It softens every outline and cushions every stone. . . .

John Burroughs

All the larger streams of uncultivated countries are mysteriously charming and beautiful, whether flowing in mountains or through swamps and plains. Their channels are interestingly sculptured, far more so than the grandest architectural works of man. The finest of the forests are usually found along their banks, and in the multitude of falls and rapids in the wilderness finds a voice. Such a river is the Hiwassee, with its surface broken to a thousand sparkling gems, and its forest walls vine-draped and flowery as Eden. And how fine the songs it sings!

John Muir

Half a mile or so downstream, I remember, we sat for a long time beside a diminutive waterfall only a foot or two high, delighting in the low music that filled the air. The water gurgled and hissed, lisped and murmured. Never before had we appreciated quite so clearly how many rushing, bubbling, liquid sounds combine to form the music of falling water. All down the river, all through the day, all through the night, the song of the running water went on and on. Light and dark are the same to a flowing stream. For it, only gravity matters.

Edwin Way Teale

I jot this mem. in a wild scene of woods and hills, where we have come to visit a waterfall. I never saw finer or more copious hemlocks, many of them large, some old and hoary. Such a sentiment to them, secretive, shaggy— what I call weather-beaten and let-alone—a rich underlay of ferns, yew sprouts and mosses, beginning to be spotted with the early summer wildflowers. Enveloping all, the monotone and liquid gurgle from the hoarse impetuous copious fall—the greenish-tawny, darkly transparent waters, plunging with velocity down the rocks, with patches of milk-white foam—a stream of hurrying amber, thirty feet wide, risen far back in the hills and woods, now rushing with volume—every hundred yards a fall, and sometimes three or four in that distance. A primitive forest, druidical, solitary and savage—not ten visitors a year—broken rocks everywhere—shade overhead, thick underfoot with leaves—a just palpable wild and delicate aroma.

Walt Whitman

The Pine-Tree

I wonder why it is that the pine has an ancient look, a suggestion in some way of antiquity? Is it because we know it to be the oldest tree? or is it not rather that its repose, its silence, its unchangeableness, suggest the past, and cause it to stand out in sharp contrast upon the background of the flitting, fugitive present? It has such a look of permanence! When growing from the rocks, it seems expressive of the same geologic antiquity as they. It has the simplicity of primitive things; the deciduous trees seem more complex, more heterogeneous; they have greater versatility, more resources. The pine has but one idea, and that is to mount heavenward by regular steps—tree of fate, tree of dark shadows and of mystery.

The pine is the tree of silence. Who was the Goddess of Silence? Look for her altars amid the pines—silence above, silence below. Pass from deciduous woods into pine woods of a windy day, and you think the day has suddenly become calm. Then how silent to the foot! One walks over a carpet of pine needles almost as noiselessly as over the carpets of our dwellings. Do these halls lead to the chambers of the great, that all noise should be banished from them? Let the designers come here and get the true pattern for a carpet—a soft yellowish brown with only a red leaf, or a bit of gray moss, or a dusky lichen scattered here and there; a background that does not weary or bewilder the eye, or insult the ground-loving foot.

John Burroughs

The waving of a forest of the giant sequoias is indescribably impressive and sublime, but the pines seem to me the best interpreters of winds. They are mighty waving goldenrods, ever in tune, singing and writing wind-music all their long century lives.

John Muir

How friendly the pine tree is to man— so docile and available as timber, and so warm and protective as shelter! Its balsam is salve to his wounds, its fragrance is long life to his nostrils; an abiding, perennial tree, tempering the climate, cool as murmuring waters in summer and like a wrapping of fur in winter.

John Burroughs

The very uprightness of the pines and maples asserts the ancient rectitude and vigor of nature. Our lives need the relief of such a background, where the pine flourishes and the jay still screams.

Henry David Thoreau

Strange that so few ever come to the woods to see how the pine lives and grows and spires, lifting its evergreen arms to the light,—to see its perfect success. . . .

Henry David Thoreau

The forests of America, however slighted by man, must have been a great delight to God; for they were the best he ever planted.

John Muir

You only need sit still long enough in some attractive spot in the woods that all its inhabitants may exhibit themselves to you by turns.

Henry David Thoreau

Seek the silent woodland where no sound of wheels is heard and nothing breaks the stillness save the singing of a bird.

Nature tells her secrets not to those who hurry by, but to those who walk with happy heart and seeing eye.

Patience Strong

Within a little more than a fortnight the woods, from bare twigs, have become a sea of verdure, and young shoots have contended with one another in the race. The leaves are unfurled all over the country. . . Shade is produced, and the birds are concealed and their economies go forward uninterruptedly, and a covert is afforded to animals generally. But thousands of worms and insects are preying on the leaves while they are young and tender. Myriads of little parasols are suddenly spread all the country over, to shield the earth and the roots of the trees from the parching heat, and they begin to flutter and rustle in the breeze.

Henry David Thoreau

In the woods, things are close to you, and you touch them and seem to interchange something with them; but upon the river, even though it be a narrow and shallow one, you are more isolated, farther removed from the soil and its attractions, and an easier prey to the unsocial demons. The long, unpeopled vistas ahead; the still, dark eddies; the endless monotone and soliloquy of the stream; the unheeding rocks basking like monsters along the shore, half out of the water, half in; a solitary heron starting up here and there, as you rounded some point, and flapping disconsolately ahead till lost to view, or standing like a gaunt specter on the umbrageous side of the mountain, his motionless form revealed against the dark green as you passed; the trees and willows and alders that hemmed you in on either side, and hid the fields and the farmhouses and the road that ran nearby—these things and others . . . cast a gloom over my spirits.

John Burroughs

The Majesty of Trees

There is a serene and settled majesty in woodland scenery that enters into the soul, and delights and elevates it, and fills it with noble inclinations. As the leaves of trees are said to absorb all noxious qualities of the air and to breathe forth a purer atmosphere, so it seems to me as if they drew from us all sordid and angry passions, and breathed forth peace and philanthropy.

There is something nobly simple and pure in a taste for the cultivation of forest trees. It argues, I think, a sweet and generous nature to have this strong relish for the beauties of vegetation and this friendship for the hardy and glorious sons of the forest. There is a grandeur of thought connected with this part of rural economy. It is, if I may be allowed the figure, the heroic line of husbandry. It is worthy of liberal, and free-born, and aspiring men. He who plants an oak, looks forward to future ages, and plants for posterity. Nothing can be less selfish than this.

Washington Irving

I Know a Wood

I know a wood where the morning air
Is sweet with silver dew,
Where dappled paths wind their secret ways
To vistas ever new;
Where fronded filigree of fern
And emerald lace of leaf
Cast intricate pattern of shadow work,
Exquisite beyond belief.

I know a wood where time stands still
On a summer afternoon,
Where mellow July and August ripe
Hold all the charms of June;
Where brambles are jewelled with purple fruit,
Where violets star the ground,
Where the spider dreams in her silken web
With bee-hum the only sound.

I know a wood where sleepy birds
Sing muted at even's hour,
Where the cares of the world seem faraway,
Where peace lends a healing power;
Where the sinking sun throws shafted beams
Of gold through ancient trees,
And the air holds a rustle of sweet good-nights
With the stilling of daytime's breeze.

Gladys Doonan

Knee-Deep in June

Tell you what I like the best—
  'Long about knee-deep in June,
'Bout the time strawberries melts
  On the vine, some afternoon
Like to jes' git out and rest,
  And not work at nothin' else!

Orchard's where I'd ruther be—
Needn't fence it in for me!
  Jes' the whole sky overhead,
And the whole airth underneath—
Sorto's so's a man kin breathe
  Like he ort, and kindo' has

Elbow room to keerlessly
  Sprawl out len'thways on the grass
    Where the shadders thick and soft
  As the kivvers on the bed
  Mother fixes in the loft
Allus, when they's company!

Jes' a-sorto' lazin, there—
  S'lazy, 'at you peek and peer
    Through the wavin' leaves above,
    Like a feller 'at's in love
  And don't know it, ner don't keer!
Ever'thing you hear and see

    Got some sorto' interest—
    Maybe find a bluebird's nest
  Tucked up there conveenently
  Fer the boy 'at's ap' to be
  Up some other apple-tree!
Watch the swallers skootin' past
'Bout as peert as you could ast;
  Er the Bob-white raise and whiz
  Where some other's whistle is.

Ketch a shadder down below,
And look up to find the crow—
Er a hawk—away up there,
'Peerantly froze in the air!
  Hear the old hen squawk, and squat
  Over ever' chick she's got,
Suddent-like—and she knows where
  That-air hawk is, well as you!
  You jes' bet yer life she do!
    Eyes a-glitterin' like glass,
    Waitin' till he makes a pass!

Pee-wees' singin', to express
  My opinion, 's second class,
Yit you'll hear 'em more er less;
  Sapsucks gittin' down to biz,
Weedin' out the lonesomeness;

Mr. Bluejay, full o' sass,
  In them base-ball clothes o' his,
Sportin' round the orchard jes'
Like he owned the premises!
  Sun out in the fields kin sizz,
But flat on yer back, I guess,
  In the shade's where glory is!
That's jes' what I'd like to do
Stiddy fer a year er two!

Plague! ef they ain't somepin' in
Work 'at kindo' goes ag'in
  My convictions—'long about
  Here in June especially!

Under some old apple-tree,
  Jes' a-restin' through and through,
I coud git along without
  Nothin' else at all to do
  Only jes' a-wishin' you
  Wuz a-gittin' there like me,
  And June was eternity!

Lay out there and try to see
Jes' how lazy you kin be!
  Tumble round and souse yer head
  In the clover-bloom, er pull
  Yer straw hat acrost yer eyes
  And peek through it at the skies,
Thinkin' of old chums 'at's dead;
  Maybe smilin' back at you
  I' betwixt the beautiful
  Clouds o' gold and white and blue!
Month a man kin railly love—
June, you know, I'm talkin' of!

March ain't never nothin' new!
Aprile's altogether too
  Brash fer me! and May—I jes'
  'Bominate its promises—
Little hints o' sunshine and
Green around the timber-land—
  A few promises, and a few
  Chip-birds, and a sprout er two,
    Drap asleep, and it turns in
    'Fore daylight and snows ag'in!

But when June comes—Clear my throat
  With wild honey! Rench my hair
In the dew! and hold my coat!
  Whoop out loud! and throw my hat!
June wants me, and I'm to spare!
Spread them shadders anywhere,
I'll git down and waller there,
  And obleeged to you at that!

James Whitcomb Riley

Summer always comes in the person of June, with a bunch of daisies on her breast and clover blossoms in her hands. A new chapter in the season is opened when these flowers appear. One says to himself, "Well, I have lived to see the daisies again and to smell the red clover." One plucks the first blossoms tenderly and caressingly. What memories are stirred in the mind by the fragrance of the one and the youthful face of the other! There is nothing else like that smell of the clover: it is the maidenly breath of summer; it suggests all fresh, buxom, rural things. A field of ruddy, blooming clover, dashed or sprinkled here and there with the snow-white of the daisies; its breath drifts into the road when you are passing; you hear the boom of bees, the voice of bobolinks, the twitter of swallows, the whistle of woodchucks; you smell wild strawberries; you see the cattle upon the hills; you see your youth, the youth of a happy farm boy, rise before you.

John Burroughs

When July comes, summer shifts into high gear. Days of hazy, shimmering heat arrive; hayloads roll in from the mowing fields; gray young starlings and new red-winged blackbirds gather in flocks and settle on the open pastures.

In July we are in a month that looks forward and backward—forward to autumn, backward to spring. Watching the new birds flocking together, seeing in them one of the earliest signs of fall, we experience each year the same feeling Thoreau recorded in his journal: "How early in the year it begins to be late!"

But at the same time that we sense this rushing onward toward the autumn, we are conscious that everywhere around us there remain evidences of the spring. We are still in the time of little things: little rabbits, newly fledged birds, sprouts of trees struggling upward, young woodchucks feeding in the meadows, tadpoles and minnows swarming in the shallows at the pond edge. We are still in the time of the new, the time of the rejuvenation of the world.

Edwin Way Teale   27

From Endymion

A thing of beauty is a joy forever:
Its loveliness increases; it will never
Pass into nothingness; but still will keep
A bower quiet for us, and a sleep
Full of sweet dreams, and health, and quiet
    breathing.
Therefore, on every morrow, are we wreathing
A flowery band to bind us to the earth,
Spite of despondence, of the inhuman dearth
Of noble natures, of the gloomy days,
Of all the unhealthy and o'er-darkened ways
Made for our searching: yes, in spite of all,
Some shape of beauty moves away the pall
From our dark spirits. Such the sun, the moon,
Trees old and young, sprouting a shady boon
For simple sheep; and such are daffodils
With the green world they live in; and clear rills
That for themselves a cooling covert make
'Gainst the hot season; the mid-forest brake,
Rich with a sprinkling of fair musk rose blooms:
And such too is the grandeur of the dooms
We have imagined for the mighty dead;
All lovely tales that we have heard or read:
And endless fountain of immortal drink,
Pouring unto us from the heaven's brink.
Nor do we merely feel these essences
For one short hour; no, even as the trees
That whisper round a temple become soon
Dear as the temple's self, so does the moon,
The passion poesy, glories infinite,
Haunt us till they become a cheering light
Unto our souls, and bound to us so fast,
That, whether there be shine, or gloom o'ercast,
They always must be with us, or we die.

John Keats

Nature does nothing merely for beauty; beauty follows as the inevitable result; and the final impression of health and finish which her works make upon the mind is owing as much to those things which are not technically called beautiful as to those which are. The former give identity to the latter. The one is to the other what substance is to form, or bone to flesh. The beauty of nature includes all that is called beautiful, as its flower; and all that is not called beautiful, as its stalk and roots.

John Burroughs

Beauty is composed of many things and never stands alone. It is part of horizons, blue in the distance, great primeval silences, knowledge of all things of the earth. It embodies the hopes and dreams of those who have gone before, including the spirit world; it is so fragile it can be destroyed by a sound or thought. It may be infinitesimally small or encompass the universe itself. It comes in a swift conception wherever nature has not been disturbed.

Sigurd F. Olson

I noticed this phenomenon early in life, during my guiding days. As soon as men forgot complexities and problems, the ancient joy took hold. Men who had never sung a note before bellowed songs into the teeth of the wind; faces that at the start showed grimness and strain soon began to relax.

Sigurd F. Olson

The tendency nowadays to wander in wildernesses is delightful to see. Thousands of tired, nerve-shaken, over-civilized people are beginning to find out that going to the mountains is going home; that wildness is a necessity; and that mountain parks and reservations are useful not only as fountains of timber and irrigating rivers, but as fountains of life. Awakening from the stupefying effects of the vice of over-industry and the deadly apathy of luxury, they are trying as best they can to mix and enrich their own little ongoings with those of nature, and to get rid of rust and disease. Briskly venturing and roaming, some are washing off sins and cobweb cares of the devil's spinning in all-day storms on mountains; sauntering in resiny pinewoods or in gentian meadow, brushing through chaparral, bending down and parting sweet, flowery sprays; tracing rivers to their sources, getting in touch with the nerves of Mother Earth; jumping from rock to rock, feeling the life of them, learning the songs of them, panting in whole-souled exercise, and rejoicing in deep, long-drawn breaths of pure wildness. This is fine and natural and full of promise.

John Muir

Back to Nature

I love to dwell in forest wild
Where giant pine trees pierce the sky;
A beauty spot where nature smiled,
A fitting place to live and die.

Where lake waves kiss the sandy beach,
The native haunt of timid deer;
A sermon only God can preach
But every human soul may hear.

The book of nature opened wide . . .
Each page some wondrous joy unfolds
To him whose conscience is his guide;
He learns the secrets nature holds.

I've played my part in life's affairs,
I'm weary of the noise and strife;
So let me put aside my cares
And live the quiet simple life.

E. F. Hayward

It is not surprising city dwellers leave their homes each weekend and head for beaches, mountains, or plains where they can recapture the feeling of timelessness. It is this need, as much as scenery or just getting out of town, that is the reason for their escape. In the process, however, they may still be so imbued with the sense of hurry and the thrill of travel

In the wilderness there is never this sense of having to move, never the feeling of boredom if nothing dramatic happens. Time moves slowly, as it should, for it is a part of beauty that cannot be hurried if it is to be understood. Without this easy flowing, life can become empty and hectic.

Sigurd F. Olson

that they actually lose what they came to find. Many tour the national parks with the major objective of getting as many park stickers as possible in the short time available, and what should have been a leisurely experience becomes a race to include all the areas within reach. When such travelers return, they are often wearier than when they started.

Sigurd F. Olson

But better than fish or game or grand scenery, or any adventure by night or day, is the wordless intercourse with rude Nature one has on these expeditions. It is something to press the pulse of our old mother by mountain lakes and streams, and know what health and vigor are in her veins, and how regardless of observation she deports herself.

John Burroughs

Let us spend one day as deliberately as Nature, and not be thrown off the track by every nutshell and mosquito's wing that falls on the rails. Let us rise early and fast, or break fast, gently and without perturbation; let company go, let the bells ring and the children cry—determined to make a day of it. Why should we knock under and go with the stream?

Let us not be upset and overwhelmed in that terrible rapid and whirlpool called a dinner, situated in the meridian shallows. Weather this danger and you are safe, for the rest of the way is downhill.

Henry David Thoreau

One has only to sit down in the woods or fields or by the shore of the river or lake, and nearly everything of interest will come round to him—the birds, the animals, the insects; and presently, after his eye has got accustomed to the place and to the light and shade, he will probably see some plant or flower that he has sought in vain for, and that is a pleasant surprise to him. So, on a large scale, the student and lover of nature has this advantage over people who gad up and down the world seeking some novelty or excitement: he has only to stay at home and see the procession pass. The great globe swings around to him like a revolving showcase; the change of the seasons is like the passage of strange and new countries; the zones of the earth, with all their beauties and marvels, pass one's door and linger long in the passing.

John Burroughs

31

Adopt the pace of nature: her secret is patience.

Ralph Waldo Emerson

Listen with Your Heart

Go out, go out I beg of you,
  And taste the beauty of the wild.
Behold the miracle of earth
  With all the wonder of a child,
Walk hand in hand with nature's god,
  Where scarlet lilies brightly flame.
Make footprints in the virgin sod,
  By some clear lake without a name.

Listen not only with your ears,
  But make your heart a listening post.
Travel above the timberline,
  Make fires on some lonely coast,
Breathe the high air of snow-crowned peaks,
  Taste fog and kelp and salty tides,
Go pitch your tent amid the pines
  Where golden sun and peace abide.

Follow the trail of moose and deer,
  The wild goose on his lonely flight,
Savor the fragrance of the wild,
  The sweetness of a northern night.
Drink deep of distance, rest your eyes
  Where centuries of peace have lain,
And let your thoughts go winging out
  Beyond the realm of man's domain.

Lay hold upon the out-of-doors
  With heart and soul and seeking brain,
You'll find the answer to all life
  Held in the sun and wind and rain.
Where'er you walk by land or sea
  The page is clear for all who seek,
If you will listen with your heart
  And let the voice of nature speak.

Edna Jaques

I have never felt lonesome, or in the least oppressed by a sense of solitude, but once, and that was a few weeks after I came to the woods, when, for an hour, I doubted if the near neighborhood of man was not essential to a serene and healthy life. To be alone was something unpleasant. But I was at the same time conscious of a slight insanity in my mood, and seemed to foresee my recovery. In the midst of a gentle rain while these thoughts prevailed, I was suddenly sensible of such sweet and beneficent society of nature, in the very pattering of the drops, and in every sound and sight across my house, an infinite and unaccountable friendliness all at once like an atmosphere sustaining me, as made the fancied advantages of human neighborhood insignificant, and I have never thought of them since. Every little pine needle expanded and swelled with sympathy and befriended me. I was so distinctly made aware of the presence of something kindred to me, even in scenes which we are accustomed to call wild and dreary, and also that the nearest of blood to me and humanest was not a person nor a villager, that I thought no place could ever be strange to me again.

Henry David Thoreau

I have had my share of solitude and know whereof I speak. It is beautiful to me, for it brings back perspective and the sense of timelessness. I come back to the friends I have left, stronger, better, and happier than when I went away. If there is writing to do, my thoughts run more smoothly than before; my perceptions and understanding of life's problems more uncluttered after the cleansing powers of solitude.

Sigurd F. Olson

Everyone needs such quiet times, some solitude to recoup his sense of perspective. One does not have to be in a canoe or in some remote wilderness. I find such times at night when I do much of my reading, but to me when solitude is part of wilderness it comes more surely and with greater meaning. Since the time when man often traveled alone, hunting and foraging, all this became part of him. It is easy to slip back into the ancient grooves of experience.

Sigurd F. Olson

That day, with white horses all the way from Shagwenaw, we had known fear too, and also the joy that comes when a run is over and you sit in some foam-laced eddy at a rapids' base, looking back. No one who has ever done that can forget the sight, the sound, and the feel of fast water or the wonder and sense of triumph.

Sigurd F. Olson

Rapids, too, are a challenge. Dangerous though they may be, treacherous and always unpredictable, no one who has known the canoe trails of the north does not love their thunder and the rush of them. No man who has portaged around white water, studied the swirls, the smooth, slick sweeps and the V's that point the way above the breaks has not wondered if he should try. Rapids can be run in larger craft, in scows and rubber boats and rafts, but it is in a canoe that one really feels the river and its power.

Is there any suspense that quite compares with that moment of commitment when the canoe heads toward the lip of a long, roaring rapids and then is taken by its unseen power? At first there is no sense of speed, but suddenly you are part of it, involved in spume and spouting rocks. Then, when there is no longer any choice and a man knows that his fate is out of hand, his is a sense of fierce abandonment when all the *voyageurs* of the past join the rapids in their shouting.

While the canoe is in the grip of the river, a man knows what detachment means; knows that, having entered the maelstrom, he is at its mercy until it has spent its strength. When through skill or luck he has gone through the snags, the reaching rocks, and the lunging billows, he needs no other accolade but the joy that he has known.

Sigurd F. Olson

The canoe gives a sense of unbounded range and freedom, unlimited movement and exploration, such as larger craft never know. . . . It is as free as the wind itself, can go wherever fancy dictates. The canoeman can camp each night in a different place, explore out-of-the-way streams and their sources, find hidden corners where no one has ever been.

Sigurd F. Olson

The movement of a canoe is like a reed in the wind. Silence is part of it, and the sounds of lapping water, bird songs, and wind in the trees. It is part of the medium through which it floats: the sky, the water, the shores.

In a canoe a man changes and the life he has lived seems strangely remote. Time is no longer of moment, for he has become part of space and freedom. What matters is that he is heading down the misty trail of explorers and *voyageurs,* with a fair wind and a chance for a good camp somewhere ahead. The future is other lakes, countless rapids and the sound of them, portages through muskeg and over the ledges.

Sigurd Olson

There is magic in the feel of a paddle and the movement of a canoe, a magic compounded of distance, adventure, solitude, and peace. The way of a canoe is the way of the wilderness and of a freedom almost forgotten. It is an antidote to insecurity, the open door to waterways of ages past and a way of life with profound and abiding satisfactions. . . .

Sigurd F. Olson

After such a voyage, the troubled and angry waters, which once had seemed terrible and not to be trifled with, appeared tamed and subdued; they had been bearded and worried in their channels, pricked and whipped into submission with the spike-pole and paddle, gone through and through with impunity, and all their spirit and their danger taken out of them, and the most swollen and impetuous rivers seemed but playthings henceforth. I began, at length, to understand the boatman's familiarity with, and contempt for, the rapids.

Henry David Thoreau

Something happens to a man when he sits before a fire. Strange stirrings take place within him and a light comes into his eyes which was not there before. An open flame suddenly changes his environment to one of adventure and romance. Even an indoor fireplace has this effect, though its owner is protected by four walls and the assurance that, should the fire go out, his thermostat will keep him warm. No matter where an open fire happens to be—in city apartments, a primitive cabin, or deep in the wilderness—it weaves its spell.

Sigurd Olson

Not the least of the charm of camping out is your campfire at night. What an artist! What pictures are boldly thrown or faintly outlined upon the canvas of the night! Every object, every attitude of your companion, is striking and memorable. You see effects and groups every moment that you would give money to be able to carry away with you in enduring form. How the shadows leap, and skulk, and hover about! Light and darkness are in perpetual tilt and warfare, with first the one unhorsed, then the other. The friendly and cheering fire, what acquaintance we make with it! We had almost forgotten there was such an element, we had so long known only its dark offspring, heat. Now we see the wild beauty uncaged and note its manner and temper. How surely it creates its own draft and sets currents going, as force and enthusiasm always will! It carves itself a chimney out of the fluid and houseless air. A friend, a ministering angel, in subjection; a fiend, a fury, a monster, ready to devour the world, if ungoverned. By day it burrows in the ashes and sleeps; at night it comes forth and sits upon its throne of rude logs, and rules the camp, a sovereign queen....

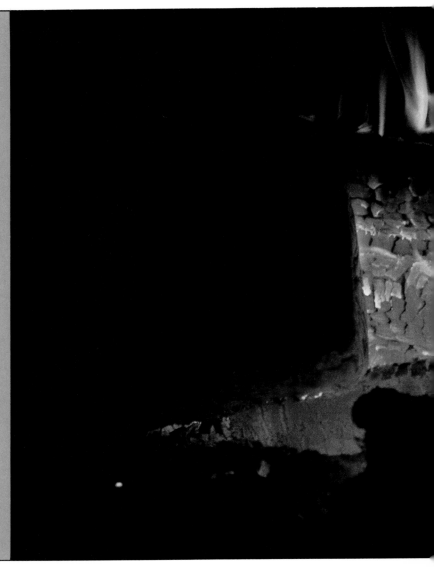

There have been countless campfires, each one different, some so blended into their backgrounds it is hard for them to emerge. But I have found when I catch even a glimmer of their almost forgotten light in the eyes of someone who shared them with me, they flame once more.

Sigurd F. Olson

What does the camper think about when lounging around the fire at night? Not much—of the sport of the day, of the big fish he lost and might have saved, of the distant settlement, of tomorrow's plans. An owl hoots off in the mountain and he thinks of him; if a wolf were to howl or a panther to scream, he would think of him the rest of the night. As it is, things flicker and hover through his mind, and he hardly knows whether it is the past or the present that possesses him. Certain it is, he feels the hush and solitude of the great forest, and, whether he will or not, all his musings are in some way cast upon that huge background of the night. Unless he is an old camper-out, there will be an undercurrent of dread or half fear. My companion said he could not help but feel all the time that there ought to be a sentinel out there pacing up and down. One seems to require less sleep in the woods, as if the ground and the untempered air rested and refreshed him sooner. The balsam and the hemlock heal his aches very quickly.

John Burroughs

Around the Campfire

Come place a log upon the fire,
    A sign of friendship true.
Then you may sit and talk with me
    And I shall talk with you.

The years have flown since we last sat
    Beside a campfire bright;
But I have longed to talk with you
    As we shall talk tonight.

I have not traveled far in miles;
    But with my questing eyes
I've found unbounded beauty waits
    Beneath these spacious skies.

I've learned to see with open mind
    The grandeur near at hand,
And all that nature gives to us
    I've tried to understand.

I do not long for distant shores
    But just to have the time
To roam about these mountain woods
    And make them really mine.

I'll place more wood upon the fire
    To keep our campsite bright,
For I am glad that you, my friend,
    Are with me here tonight.

Vernice Moore Gilfilen

Our big fire, heaped high with resiny logs and branches, is blazing like a sunrise, gladly giving back the light slowly sifted from the sunbeams of centuries of summers; and in the glow of that old sunlight how impressively surrounding objects are brought forward in relief against the outer darkness! Grasses, larkspurs, columbines, lilies, hazel bushes, and the great trees form a circle around the fire like thoughtful spectators, gazing and listening with human-like enthusiasm.

John Muir

Our camp-fire at night served more purposes than one; from its embers and flickering shadows, Uncle Nathan read us many a tale of his life in the woods. They were the same old hunter's stories, except that they evidently had the merit of being strictly true, and hence were not very thrilling or marvelous.

John Burroughs

Once a man has known the warmth and companionship there, once he has tasted the thrill of stories of the chase with the firelight in his eyes, he has made contact with the past, recaptured some of the lost wonder of his early years and some of the sense of mystery of his forebears. He has reforged a link in his memory that was broken when men abandoned the life of the nomad and moved from the forests, plains, and mountains to the security of villages. Having rebridged the gap, he swiftly discovers something he had lost: a sense of belonging to the earth and to his kind. When that happens, he reaches back beyond his own life experiences to a time when existence was simple.

Sigurd F. Olson

As darkness came on, the rumbling increased, and the mountains and the woods and the still air were such good conductors of sound that the ear was vividly impressed. One seemed to feel the enormous convolutions of the clouds in the deep and jarring tones of the thunder. The coming of night in the woods is alone peculiarly impressive, it is doubly so when out of the darkness comes such a voice as this. But we fed the fire the more industriously, and piled the logs high, and kept the gathering gloom at bay by as large a circle of light as we could command.

John Burroughs

Our camp was amid a dense grove of second growth of white pine on the eastern shore, where, for one, I found a most admirable cradle in a little depression outside of the tent, carpeted with pine needles, in which to pass the night. The camper-out is always in luck if he can find, sheltered by the trees, a soft hole in the ground, even if he has a stone for a pillow. The earth must open its arms a little for us even in life, if we are to sleep well upon its bosom.

John Burroughs

Camp life is a primitive affair, no matter how many conveniences you have, and things of the mind keep pretty well in the background.

John Burroughs

Music of fire . . . Freedom to think . . . The smell of burning pitch-pine wood . . . Smoke from the campfire . . . The expectation to explore . . . Letting the sun be my wristwatch . . . The gentle warmth of tender, early morning light . . . Conversation with new-made friends . . . A camera in my lap . . . Pleasure in my nap . . . The lines of the trees . . . Splendor of blue sky . . . An insect passing by . . . The joy of luxurious leisure . . . The distant clang of horseshoe stakes . . . The art of living in the present, but also thoughts of the remembered past . . . The quietude of heart at ease . . . Ashes in the breeze.

Larry Roger Clark

When one breaks camp in the morning, he turns back again and again to see what he has left. Surely, he feels, he has forgotten something; what is it? But it is only his own sad thoughts and musings he has left, the fragment of his life he has lived there. Where he hung his coat on the tree, where he slept on the boughs, where he made his coffee or broiled his trout over the coals, where he drank again and again at the little brown pool in the spring run, where he looked long and long up into the whispering branches overhead, he has left what he cannot bring away with him—the flame and the ashes of himself.

John Burroughs

We broke camp early in the morning, and with our blankets strapped to our backs and rations in our pockets for two days, set out along an ancient and in places an obliterated bark road that followed and crossed and recrossed tne stream. The morning was bright and warm, but the wind was fitful and petulant, and I predicted rain. What a forest solitude our obstructed and dilapidated woodroad led us through!

John Burroughs

39

To recapture the spirit of any era you must follow old trails, gathering from the earth itself the feelings and challenges of those who trod them long ago. The landscape and way of life may have changed, but the same winds blow on waterways, plains, and mountains, the rains, snows, and sun beat down, and the miles are just as long.

Sigurd F. Olson

The Knapsack Trail

I like the wide and common road
Where all may walk at will,
The worn and rutted country road
That runs from hill to hill;

I like the road through pastures green
Worn by homecoming feet
Of lowing kine and barefoot boy
Where twilight shadows meet.

But I like best the Knapsack Trail
Wherein my heart and I
May walk and talk in quietness
With angels passing by.

The lonely trail through forest dim
That leads to God-knows-where,
That winds from tree to spotted tree
Till sudden—we are there!

Edwin Osgood Grover

It is surprising how much room there is in nature, if a man will follow his proper path. In these broad fields, in these extensive woods, on this stretching river, I never meet a walker. Passing behind the farmhouses, I see no man out. Perhaps I do not meet so many men as I should have met three centuries ago, when the Indian hunter roamed these woods. I enjoy the retirement and solitude of an early settler. Men have cleared some of the earth, which no doubt is an advantage to the walker.

Henry David Thoreau

The human body is a steed that goes freest and longest under a light rider, and the lightest of all riders is a cheerful heart. Your sad or morose or embittered or preoccupied heart settles heavily into the saddle, and the poor beast, the body, breaks down the first mile. Indeed, the heaviest thing in the world is a heavy heart. Next to that, the most burdensome to the walker is a heart not in perfect sympathy and accord with the body—a reluctant or unwilling heart. The horse and rider must not only both be willing to go the same way, but the rider must lead the way and infuse his own lightness and eagerness into the steed. Herein is no doubt our trouble, and one reason of the decay of the noble art in this country. We are unwilling walkers. We are not innocent and simplehearted enough to enjoy a walk. . . .

John Burroughs

For countless thousands of years men have followed such trails. It is instinctive to pack across them, and you bend and weave, adjust your weight and balance, do all the things your subconscious experience tells you to do without realizing exactly what is happening. In the low places your feet feel for the rocks and tussocks of grass, for the sunken logs that keep you from bogging down. You approach them as a horse approaches a bridge, with the same awareness of danger. Over the rocks and beside a rapids, where a slip might plunge you into a torrent or over a cliff, your feet are your eyes as they have always been where the going is rough.

Sigurd F. Olson

Song of the Open Road

Afoot and lighthearted I take to the open road,
Healthy, free, the world before me,
The long brown path before me leading wherever I choose.

Henceforth I ask not good fortune, I myself am good fortune,
Henceforth I whimper no more, postpone no more, need nothing,
Done with indoor complaints, libraries, querulous criticisms,
Strong and content I travel the open road.

The earth, that is sufficient,
I do not want the constellations any nearer,
I know they are very well where they are,
I know they suffice for those who belong to them.

The earth expanding right hand and left hand,
The picture alive, every part in its best light,
The music falling in where it is wanted, and stopping where it is
    not wanted,
The cheerful voice of the public road, the gay fresh sentiment of
    the road.

O highway I travel, do you say to me, "Do not leave me"?
Do you say, "Venture not—if you leave me you are lost"?
Do you say, "I am already prepared, I am well-beaten and undenied,
    adhere to me"?

O public road, I say back I am not afraid to leave you, yet I love you,
You express me better than I can express myself,
You shall be more to me than my poem.

I think heroic deeds were all conceived in the open air, and all
    free poems also;
I think I could stop here myself and do miracles;
I think whatever I shall meet on the road I shall like, and
    whoever beholds me shall like me;
I think whoever I see must be happy.

Walt Whitman

I yearn for those old, meandering, dry, uninhabited roads which lead away from town, which lead us away from temptation, which conduct to the outside of earth, over its uppermost crust; where you may forget in what country you are travelling, where no farmer can complain that you are treading down his grass, no gentleman who has recently constructed a seat in the country that you are trespassing; on which you can go off at half-cock and wave adieu to the village; along which you may travel like a pilgrim, going nowhither. Where travellers are not too often to be met; where my spirit is free; where the walls and the fences are not cared for; where your head is more in heaven than your feet on earth; which have long reaches where you can see the approaching traveller half a mile off and be prepared for him; not so luxuriant a soil as to attract men; some root and stump fences which do not need attention; where travellers have no occasion to stop, but pass along and leave you to your thoughts. Where it makes no odds which way you face, whether you are going or coming, whether it is morning or evening, midnoon or midnight; where earth is cheap enough by being public; where you can walk and think with least obstruction, there being nothing to measure progress by. Where you can pace when your breast is full, and cherish your moodiness; where you are not false in relations with men, are not dining nor conversing with them; by which you may go to the uttermost parts of the earth. It is wide enough, wide as the thoughts it allows to visit you.

Henry David Thoreau

Now I yearn for one of those old, meandering, dry, uninhabited roads, which lead away from town, which lead us away from temptation, which conduct to the outside of earth, over its uppermost crust; where you may forget in what country you are traveling. . . .

Henry David Thoreau

It is not the walking merely, it is keeping yourself in tune for a walk, in the spiritual and bodily condition in which you can find entertainment and exhilaration in so simple and natural a pastime. You are eligible to any good fortune when you are in the condition to enjoy a walk. When the air and the water taste sweet to you, how much else will taste sweet! When the exercise of your limbs affords you pleasure, and the play of your senses upon the various objects and shows of nature quickens and stimulates your spirit, your relation to the world and to yourself is what it should be—simple and direct and wholesome. . . .

John Burroughs

How much more one enjoys a countryside when walking through it! The sounds of the road, the constant sense of the mechanical detract from the complete enjoyment that means recreation and reversal of the type of experience we are accustomed to in everyday life. So often holidays are merely an extension of the identical influences we seek to escape. The fact that we have changed the scene makes little difference unless there is the compensating fact of quiet.

One does not have to be alone to enjoy silence. It has often been said that the ability to enjoy it with others is the mark of friendship and understanding. Only when people are strangers do they feel obliged to be entertaining. Where there is agreement and appreciation, silence is no bar to mutual enjoyment. When I have been alone in quiet places, I have often wished someone could share it and make the experience even richer and more complete.

Sigurd Olson

What more luxuriant than a clover field. The poorest soil that is covered with it looks incomparably fertile. This is perhaps the most characteristic feature of June, resounding with the hum of insects, such a blush on the fields. The rude health of the sorrel cheek has given place to the blush of clover. Painters are wont, in their pictures of Paradise, to strew the field too thickly with flowers. There should be moderation in all things. Though we love flowers we do not want them so thick under our feet that we cannot walk without treading on them. But a clover field in bloom is some excuse for them.

Henry David Thoreau

How satisfactory is the fragrance of this flower! It is the emblem of purity. It reminds me of a young country maiden. It is just so simple and unproved. Wholesome as the odor of the cow. It is not a highly refined odor, but merely a fresh youthful morning sweetness. It is merely the unalloyed sweetness of the earth and the water; a fair opportunity and field for life; like its petals, uncolored by any experience; a simple maiden on her way to school, her face surrounded by a white ruff. But how quickly it becomes the prey of insects!

Henry David Thoreau

A pretty sight! Where I sit in the shade—a warm day, the sun shining from cloudless skies, the forenoon well advanced—I look over a ten-acre field of luxuriant clover hay (the second crop)—the livid-ripe red blossoms and dabs of August brown thickly spotting the prevailing dark green. Over all flutter myriads of light yellow butterflies, mostly skimming along the surface, dipping and oscillating, giving a curious animation to the scene. The beautiful, spiritual insects! Straw-colored Psyches! Occasionally one of them leaves his mates and mounts, perhaps spirally, perhaps in a straight line in the air, fluttering up, up, till literally out of sight. In the lane as I came along just now I noticed one spot, ten feet square or so, where more than a hundred had collected, holding a revel, a gyration dance, or butterfly good time, winding and circling, down and across, but always keeping within the limits. The little creatures have come out all of a sudden the last few days, and are now very plentiful.

Walt Whitman

The pasture thistle, though past its prime, is quite common, and almost every flower where-ever you meet with it, has one or more bumblebees on it, clambering over its mass of florets. Now that flowers are rarer, almost every one of whatever species has bees or butter-flies upon it.

Henry David Thoreau

Sweet clover, unlike spiderwort, depends upon bees for its fertilization. Tall clumps of it grow along the path in the abandoned field. The blossoms are small, and at a passing glance seem insignificant, but they distill a heady perfume that makes up for their lack of size.

This perfume gives a feeling of delight when inhaled by human nostrils and creates a scented path that the bees can follow to the source of the nectar. When the flower bud first appears, the pistil is confined within a sheath, under spring tension. A bee's tongue probing for the nectar touches a trigger that releases the spring. The pistil springs erect, scattering grains of pollen on its liberator. These are then carried by the bee to the adjoining flowers, cross-fertilizing them, making payment for the nectar it has received. If the pistil is not released, the flower withers. Without the assistance of the bee there would be no sweet clover.

Wallace Kirkland

45

This is the very dead of summer. I am not sure that I ever heard just that phrase before, but I don't see why not. Surely, it describes at least the impression that August creates as she slumbers, replete and satisfied. Spring was a fever and autumn will be a regret, but this is the month too aware of its own successful achievement to be more than barely sentient. The growth which continues seems without effort, like the accumulation of fat. If nature is ever purely vegetative, it is now. She is but barely conscious.

The season of seed and fruit lies just ahead, but it is already assured and inevitable. The epoch of competition and doubt is past, the weeks when the individual did not know whether or not he was one of those who would get along in the world. The survivors are complacent; the coming months of retrenchment and death are too far away to cast a shadow, and it is at this time if ever that nature is bourgeois. At least, August is the month when the solid and the domestic triumph, when the prudent come into their own. The very birds, whose springtime was devoted to love and music, are now responsible parents who have forgotten how to sing. The early flowers of the woods waved their brief blossoms and are forgotten, but the roadsides and the fields are taken over now by the strong, coarse, and confident weeds.

John Burroughs

Nature has, for the most part, lost her delicate tints in August. She is tanned, hirsute, freckled, like one long exposed to the sun. Her touch is strong and vivid. The coarser,

Queen's Lace

Fragile and lovely as old lace,
    But just a roadside weed;
Tall and slender in regal grace,
    And faithful to its breed.
Ever growing loosely wild,
    With the pose of Nature's child

Queen's lace, so delicate and whi
    Along the countryside,
Is a lovely queenly sight
    Resplendent as a bride,
A flower no one can ever tame,
    Wild and pretty as its name.

Like majesty on her throne
    Dressed in royal robe,
With natural beauty all her own,
    With no problems left to probe
Except the one of duty:
    To give the world her beauty.

Edith H. Shan

commoner wayside flowers now appear—vervain, eupatorium, mimulus, the various mints, asters, goldenrod, thistles, fireweed, mulleins, motherwort, catnip, blueweed, turtlehead, sunflowers, clematis, evening primrose, lobelia, gerardia, and, in the marshes of the lower Hudson, marshmallows, and vast masses of the purple loosestrife. Mass and intensity take the place of delicacy and furtiveness. The spirit of Nature has grown bold and aggressive; it is rank and coarse; she flaunts her weeds in our faces. She wears a thistle on her bosom.

John Burroughs

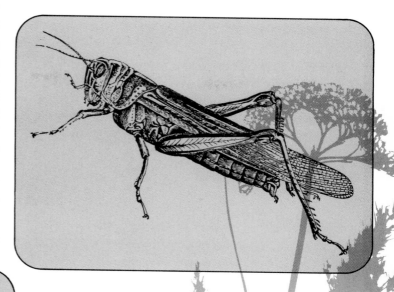

When we lay down, there was apparently not a mosquito in the woods; but the "no-see-ems," as Thoreau's Indian aptly named the midges, soon found us out and, after the fire had gone down, annoyed us much. My hands and wrists suddenly began to smart and itch in a most unaccountable manner. . . .

John Burroughs

The first mosquito of the night sounded the call to arms—to arms, to legs, to face, to neck, to any part of the anatomy that was exposed. The call was picked up by a host of others, and they all rallied to it. On swiftly moving wings, each mosquito brought an empty stomach. Connected to each was a hypodermic needle, sharpened to pierce my skin, and if I remained outside, countless mosquito stomachs would be filled with my blood.

With memories of past night assaults, I waved my handkerchief, in token of a white flag of surrender, and sadly went indoors.

Wallace Kirkland

Mosquitoes multiply rapidly. Some species can produce a new generation in two weeks. The eggs hatch in forty-eight hours; the larvae mature in seven days; the final pupal stage lasts for two. Two days after a female emerges, she can broadcast signals for a mate, locate blood for nourishing her eggs, and lay as many as three hundred.

Wallace Kirkland

Seedy monotones of locust, or sounds of katydid—I hear the latter at night, and the other both day and night, I thought the morning and evening warble of birds delightful, but I find I can listen to these strange insects with just as much pleasure. A single locust is now heard near noon from a tree two hundred feet off, as I write—a long whirring, continued, quite loud noise graded in distinct whirls, or swinging circles, increasing in strength and rapidity up to a certain point, and then a fluttering, quietly tapering fall. Each strain is continued from one to two minutes. The locust song is very appropriate to the scene—gushes, has meaning, is masculine, is like some fine old wine, not sweet, but far better than sweet.

Walt Whitman

There are more than forty orders of the animal kingdom and two of the plant world that possess the power of producing light. Of them all the most famous is the firefly. Two thousand or more species of these luminous beetles have been described in the world. Most of them inhabit the tropics. About fifty species live in the United States. The peak of their display in North America usually comes late in June and early in July. It is then that the galaxies of their winking lights, tracing innumerable glowing lines on the dark, rise across meadows and marshlands to form one of the magical ingredients of the summer.

Edwin Way Teale

A noiseless patient spider,
I mark'd where on a little promontory it stood isolated,
Mark'd how to explore the vacant vast surrounding,
It launch'd forth filament, filament, filament, out of itself,
Ever unreeling them, ever tirelessly speeding them.

And you O my soul where you stand,
Surrounded, detached, in measureless oceans of space,
Ceaselessly musing, venturing, throwing,
Seeking the spheres to connect them,
Till the bridge you will need be form'd,
Till the ductile anchor hold,
Till the gossamer thread you fling
Catch somewhere, O my soul.

Walt Whitman

The spider families all have the gift of genius. Of what ingenious devices and arts are they masters! How wide their range! They spin, they delve, they jump, they fly. They are the original spinners. They have probably been on their job since carboniferous times, many millions of years before man took up the art. And they can spin a thread so fine that science makes the astonishing statement that it would take four million of them to make a thread the caliber of one of the hairs of our head—a degree of delicacy to which man can never hope to attain.

John Burroughs

It is on the dewy August mornings that one notices the webs of the little spiders in the newly mown meadows. They look like gossamer napkins spread out upon the grass—thousands of napkins far and near. The farmer looks upon it as a sign of rain; but the napkins are there every day; only a heavier dew makes them more pronounced one morning than another.

John Burroughs

The early morning was set aside for spiders. All that had spun webs upon the tree and on the bushes below it returned to spin again. Each web was outlined by the drops of dew. The rising sun, shining on them, turned them into pearls, and as the heat increased, the pearls changed into vapor, rising as jeweled incense to the tree.

Wallace Kirkland

THE GOOD OLD SUMMERTIME

Summer Memories

As summertime draws to a close
I sit and reminisce,
Remembering the joy it brought,
The hours filled with bliss.

How anxiously I waited for
Each warm and sunny day
To bring forth all its wonders
In a lovely, magic way.

My heart was quite enchanted
By the beauty everywhere;
The hills and fields were fairylands,
Sweet and green and fair.

The azure sky, the fluffy clouds,
Each flower bright and gay,

Were gifts I fondly treasure
In my memory today.

The seashore too, held wondrous charm
Where water kissed the sands;
'Twas there I'd launch my ship of dreams
To far-off mystic lands.

And the fireflies of evening,
Like tiny lamps of gold
Winging through the starry night,
Were delightful to behold.

Though summertime is ending,
It will never quite depart,
Because its precious scenes
Will always live within my heart.

LaVerne P. Larson

By the turn of the century our country had settled down, grown up and prospered—giving people more time to be sociable. Transporation had become easier, making summertime a time to get away, see the countryside and picnic with family and friends.

The Fourth of July offered a perfect opportunity for such outings. Many people gathered in public parks where they were surrounded by bustling activity and merriment. Bands played tunes like "Old Mill Stream," "Apple Blossom Time" or "The Sidewalks of New York." The men gathered to hear politicians make speeches, while the women busily spread out the delicious items they had prepared. Young boys would sneak off to light Roman candles or whole strings of lady crackers. Later, after the picnic supper, the entire family enjoyed a show of exploding fireworks. This was a fitting finale for a happy, fun-filled day.

Independence Day was also a time for family reunions. Several days were needed to prepare the food, since no picnic was complete without old-fashioned baked beans, ham or fried chicken, potato salad, freshly baked bread, pickles, lemonade and layer cake. On the day of the reunion they all gathered in the country, on the family farm if there was one, bringing the food they had prepared. Whether the picnic was held in the city or in the country, the events on the Fourth of July would become cherished memories, brightening conversations in the months to come.

Algene Carrier

An Old-Fashioned Fourth

Give me an old-fashioned Fourth of July
When brilliant rockets illumined the sky;
When days seemed much longer and life was supreme,
And flying through space was a child's lofty dream.

The American flags hung high on each porch
And glowed in the sun like a freedom-land torch;
When an old Model T was a much-treasured prize,
And we blissfully listened to men harmonize.

When phonographs wailed the old-fashioned tunes,
And relatives gathered to exchange family news;
With horseshoes a game, and TV unknown,
And porch swings a must, ice cream made at home.

Then, feet served their purpose and cars were quite rare,
And life rolled along at a pace we could bear.
Give me an old-fashioned Fourth of July
And the holiday thrill as we watched rockets fly.

This is all wishful thinking from life's looking glass
Where we reach out to touch good old days that are past.

Helen Whiteman Shick

Small lads with hoarded firecrackers,
Girls in their best array,
Speeches and family get-togethers,
Air of a holiday.

Ice cream made in an old-style freezer
With many an arm-aching crank.
Cakes and salads, delicious chicken,
Melons cooling by the old creek bank.

Tables blowing with puffs of bunting,
A stand where speeches will soon be made.
Is that a band I hear in the distance?
Of course, it's part of the big parade.

Horses champing and skittishly stepping,
Wild-eyed because of the glare and noise;
Secret meetings, plots a-cooking
Between a band of mischievous boys.

And after the marching and speeches, what?
Why, the old dinner bell rings out,
And the food piled high on the groaning tables
Brings admiring glances and many a shout.

Then at night in the quiet and friendly dark
The lightning bugs run and hide,
For every sparkler and Roman candle
Explodes all over the countryside.

And those who have had the privilege
Of enjoying old-time demonstrations,
Are envied by all who have never known
Those Fourth of July celebrations.

Eleanor Elkins

Prize Outing

The nicest kind of outing
On a sunny summer day,
Is a real old-fashioned picnic
In the countryside so gay.

Birds sing pretty melodies
From treetops green that tower
Above the pleasant meadows,
Lush with grass and flower.

Tiny woodland creatures
Peek eagerly to see
Picnic preparations,
And keep watch constantly.

Sunbeams dance around you
With merry rays of gold,
While all of nature's beauties
Magically unfold.

A picnic is a pleasure,
Simple, sweet and gay,
Giving hearts great happiness
On a sunny summer day.

LaVerne P. Larson

Picnic Memories

Oh, turn back the time to yesteryear
When the century and we were young.
Let's think of things we used to do
And sing the songs that were sung.

Remember the Sunday School picnics?
A summer event every year
With a ball game and prizes for races . . .
(How we hoped that the day would be clear!)

The tables were loaded with goodies . . .
Sandwiches, pickles and rolls,
And beans with pork and molasses
And salads in giant-sized bowls.

There was plenty of pink lemonade,
More cakes than we ever could eat;
And then came the watermelon,
A special summertime treat!

Then the men began to play horseshoes,
The young folks all paired off and walked;
The babies took naps on their blankets,
And the ladies just sat there and talked.

The children went looking for berries,
And some dared to play in the creek,
But no matter what we were doing
The day always ended too quick.

We sang as we rode slowly homeward
With the daylight fading away,
And some of those old-time favorites
Are loved and remembered today.

Harriet Whipple

53

The Bandstand in the Park

Remember those days when pastimes were simple and leisure summer afternoons were whiled away at concerts in the park . . .

There was the soft sighing sound of the wind in the trees that mingled gently with the sounds of the people as they gathered. First the band members would arrive, setting up amid the metallic clink of instruments, softly spoken words and the scuffling of their feet against the old wood floor of the bandstand. Quiet, busy sounds.

And then, right on their heels, the sounds of the children of the town streaming into the park with exuberant shouts and whistles as they ran on ahead of their folks, calling out each other's names and darting into leafy bowers for games of hide-and-seek.

Now, coming more quietly behind, the voices of the townsfolk themselves were heard as they gathered slowly before the bandstand, saying hello and exchanging bits of gossip with neighbor and friend while their eyes searched

out their children in the crowd. Dressed in their Sunday best they slowly settled on the green wooden benches lined up before the band.

"Tap, tap." The bandleader rapped them to attention. And then with a smile and a jaunty bow he turned quickly on his heel, gave a magnificent sweep with his baton and the quiet afternoon suddenly exploded with the sound of one of Sousa's marches!

How that music rang out on the sweet summer air, rolling out across the green, bounding to the treetops, filling all the sky! Instantly a hundred hearts became as one and feet tapped, faces smiled and shoulders swayed as the people were caught up in the rhythm and the beauty of that music in the park.

Family Reunion

Grandpas, brothers, aunts and cousins . . .
Here they gather by the dozens,
More than eager each to tell
If the past year served him well.
Each for reasons of his own
Never would have stayed alone,
Away from what the crowd would say
If he ignored Reunion Day!

Some would come to show a skill;
More, declining . . . firm of will,
Insist reunions are to visit,
Or to whisper, "Now, who is it?"
Of a nephew grown most tall,
Or of a baby, pink and small.
Once a year is time, they feel,
To get clan ties on even keel!

Ball games, horeshoes, what-have-you!
Swimming, boating, lots to do,
Things vacation advertises,
Plus a number of surprises;
Like small cousins' altercations,
Or the politics of nations.
But the day is one for pleasure
And each member gets full measure.

On one point they all agree . . .
Mealtime suits the family!
Trying aunts' new recipes;
Criticizing, if they please.
By the time the day is done
Exhaustion reaches everyone.
But family plans are very clear
To return this time next year.

Marian Benedict Manwell

Meanwhile the children played and shouted and raced noisily about. There was the loud, long squeal of protest from the old hand pump whenever someone sought a drink, and here and there a squirrel scolded from the treetops; but they were just noises in the background, to be sure. For as if not hearing them at all the band played gaily on, not missing a single beat. Melody after melody rolled through those summer afternoons and every heart and soul found happiness in the music of each tune.

On and on it went, the march and then a polka and then a march again, interspersed with roars of applause that burst forth at each song's end. How sweet was that summer afternoon as overhead the sun curved slowly across the sky, shadows began to lengthen, and then the day began to die.

Yet the music lingered on and, softened by the shadows, the marches gradually gave way to the romantic little melodies popular in that day. The wind grew just a bit more chill and the sky a bit more blue, and sweethearts, sitting closer now, sometimes sneaked a kiss or two. Grandma patted Grandpa's knee and smiled up at him and Dad even put his arm around Mom, her waist still girlishly slim.

A hundred little romances went with the music as it grew dark and a hundred happy people were gathered round that bandstand in the park.

Donna Lebrecht

Baseball Memories

There is a corner lot on our street
That holds memories for us all,
Where we gathered oh, so often,
For a real good game of ball.

And happy were the faces
That played on either side,
Hoping so to get a home run
That would help to turn the tide.

Now the years have traveled onward
And we're all grown up, you see,
But ever dear to every heart
Is the "sand lot" memory.

I think God blessed our ball field
Through those years with special love,
For we kids found so much happiness
In a bat, a ball, and glove.

LaVerne P. Larson

Casey at the Bat

The outlook wasn't brilliant for the Mudville nine that day;
The score stood four to two, with but one inning more to play;
And so, when Cooney died at first, and Barrows did the same,
A sickly silence fell upon the patrons of the game.

A straggling few got up to go in deep despair. The rest
Clung to the hope which springs eternal in the human breast;
They thought, if only Casey could but get a whack, at that,
They'd put up even money now, with Casey at the bat.

But Flynn preceded Casey, as did also Jimmy Blake,
And the former was a pudding and the latter was a fake;
So upon that stricken multitude grim melancholy sat,
For there seemed but little chance of Casey's getting to the bat.

But Flynn let drive a single, to the wonderment of all,
And Blake, the much despised, tore the cover off the ball;
And when the dust had lifted, and they saw what had occurred,
There was Jimmy safe on second, and Flynn a-hugging third.

Then from the gladdened multitude went up a joyous yell,
It bounded from the mountain top, and rattled in the dell;
It struck upon the hillside, and recoiled upon the flat;
For Casey, mighty Casey, was advancing to the bat.

There was ease in Casey's manner as he stepped into his place,
There was pride in Casey's bearing, and a smile on Casey's face;
And when, responding to the cheers, he lightly doffed his hat,
No stranger in the crowd could doubt 'twas Casey at the bat.

Ten thousand eyes were on him as he rubbed his hands with dirt,
Five thousand tongues applauded when he wiped them on his shirt;
Then while the writhing pitcher ground the ball into his hip,
Defiance gleamed in Casey's eye, a sneer curled Casey's lip.

And now the leather-covered sphere came hurtling through the air,
And Casey stood a-watching it in haughty grandeur there;
Close by the sturdy batsman the ball unheeded sped.
"That ain't my style," said Casey. "Strike one," the umpire said.

From the benches, black with people, there went a muffled roar,
Like the beating of the storm-waves on a stern and distant shore;
"Kill him! kill the umpire!" shouted someone on the stand.
And it's likely they'd have killed him had not Casey raised his hand.

With a smile of Christian charity, great Casey's visage shone;
He stilled the rising tumult; he bade the game go on.
He signalled to the pitcher, and once more the spheroid flew,
But Casey still ignored it, and the umpire said, "Strike two."

"Fraud!" cried the maddened thousands, and the echo answered, "Fraud!"
But a scornful look from Casey,and the audience was awed;
They saw his face grow stern and cold, they saw his muscles strain,
And they knew that Casey wouldn't let that ball go by again.

The sneer is gone from Casey's lips; his teeth are clenched in hate;
He pounds with cruel violence his bat upon the plate.
And now the pitcher holds the ball; and now he lets it go;
And now the air is shattered by the force of Casey's blow.

Oh! somewhere in this favored land the sun is shining bright;
The band is playing somewhere, and somewhere hearts are light;
And somewhere men are laughing, and somewhere children shout;
But there is no joy in Mudville—mighty Casey has struck out.

Ernest Lawrence Thayer

A Child Once More

Exciting posters everywhere,
Ablaze in gold and red,
Arrival day for circus set,
Remember how they read?

The day of days arrived at last,
The town was all astir;
Such grand events to towns like ours,
But now and then occurred.

Far down the street, if you'll recall,
A trumpet sang so gay;
Before the band a herald rode
Astride a dapple-gray.

And close behind, the circus clown,
His garments patched and pied,
A look so sad and woebegone,
His little dog beside.

How horses pranced, they fairly danced,
Their trappings all ashine;
The camels, too, and elephants,
Their tails they held in line.

At Main Street's end the big top stood,
The sideshows gathered near.
Like Noah's ark, the animals went
Inside and disappeared.

The rings grew alive with wonder,
With milk-white steeds and clowns,
With snarling cats and elephants
And maids in spangled gowns.

And far above, the acrobats
Their daring deeds perform;
The tightrope acts, and high trapeze
Receive acclaim . . . a storm.

To eyes of youth, what wonderment
The circus holds in store;
To man, from age, a brief reprieve
To be a child once more.

Charles Ruggles Fox

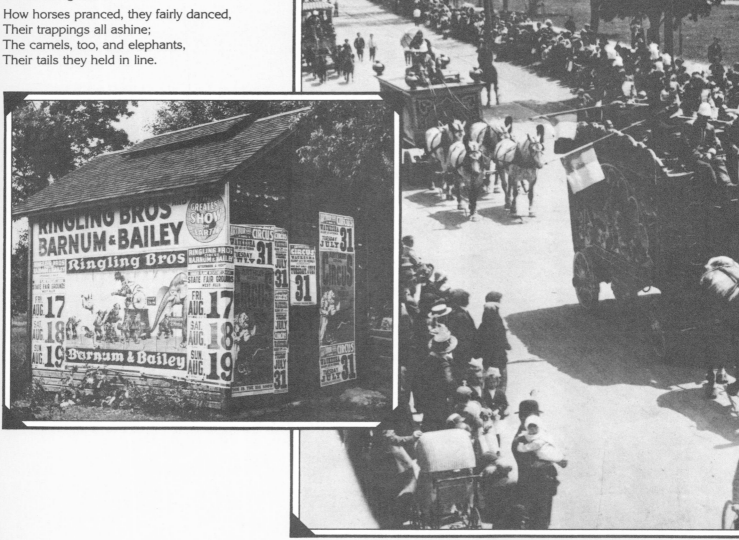

The Circus-Day Parade

Oh, the Circus-Day Parade!
  How the bugles played and played!
And how the glossy horses tossed
  their flossy manes and neighed,
As the rattle and the rhyme
  of the tenor-drummer's time
Filled all the hungry hearts of us
  with melody sublime!

How the grand bandwagon shone
  with a splendor all its own,
And glittered with a glory
  that our dreams had never known!
And how the boys behind,
  high and low of every kind,
Marched in unconscious capture,
  with a rapture undefined!

How the horsemen, two and two,
  with their plumes of white and blue,
And crimson, gold and purple,
  nodding by at me and you,
Waved the banners that they bore,
  as the Knights in days of yore,
Till our glad eyes gleamed
  and glistened like the spangles
  that they wore!

How the graceless-graceful stride
  of the elephant was eyed,
And the capers of the little horse
  that cantered at his side!
How the shambling camels, tame
  to the plaudits of their fame,
With listless eyes came silent,
  masticating as they came.

How the cages jolted past,
  with each wagon battened fast,
And the mystery within it
  only hinted of at last
From the little grated square
  in the rear, and nosing there
The snout of some strange animal
  that sniffed the outer air!

And, last of all, The Clown,
  making mirth for all the town,
With his lips curved ever upward
  And his eyebrows ever down,
And his chief attention paid
  to the little mule that played
A tattoo on the dashboard
  with his heels, in the Parade.

Oh! the Circus-Day Parade!
  How the bugles played and played!
And how the glossy horses tossed
  their flossy manes and neighed,
As the rattle and the rhyme
  of the tenor-drummer's time
Filled all the hungry hearts of us
  with melody sublime!

James Whitcomb Riley

Circus Time

How well I remember circus time
When the tents were brought to town,
And the roads were dry from a molten sky,
And the fields were turning brown.

I'll always remember how gay we were;
We cared not that it was warm,
But we watched the sky with an eagle eye
Lest there be an electric storm.

Mother starched our best white dresses
And braided our long straight hair.
We could hardly wait to go through the gate
And pay the usual fare.

Pink lemonade and popcorn,
Elephants standing in rows,
Lions and tigers in cages
And acrobats putting on shows.

All those things I remember,
The parade and the pranks of the clown.
Old folks grew young with the children
When the circus came to town.

Harriet Feltham

The Country Fair

The night before I would take out
My red plaid dress and well-greased shoes,
My hand-knit hose, and all the clothes,
And both the ribbons I would use.
And in my unbleached cotton gown,
I'd tightly braid my heavy hair.
Sleep stayed away, because next day
We all were going to the fair.

But when the milk in bright tin pans
Was set upon the cellar floor,
And when we'd spread each cornhusk bed,
And done was everybody's chore,
Dad brought around the spanking rig.
The team pranced gaily, unaware
The day was bright, the world all right,
For we were going to the fair.

Along the eight slow miles that lay
Before we reached our place of dreams,
The neighbors rode, and each abode
Turned out its share of rigs and teams.

And after what seemed endless hours
We came to wonder and to stare.
Our goal we gained, with joy unfeigned,
We tied the team and saw the fair.

The popcorn balls, the gay balloons,
I treasure yet in memory;
And when I learned that we had earned
A prize, and all the world could see
The biggest pumpkin of them all,
And I could read Dad's name and share
The happy fame of that proud name,
No wonder that I loved the fair.

The girls who rode the big balloon
And rose through such a dizzy space
Felt just as I, when by and by,
We had to leave that magic place.
My drop to earth was such a shock
I longed to cry, but did not dare.
Mom, always kind, said, "Never mind,
Next year there'll be another fair."

Anne Campbell

The Carnival

Look, there are just so many people;
   It's a great tremendous crowd.
The carnival grounds seem to be moving
   With a spirit of laughter endowed.

Noise, commotion and bustling about,
   Gay laughter, loud screams of delight,
In a setting all gleaming and glittery,
   Lights twinkle everywhere bright.

Processions, concessions, creations for fun,
   The midway's a brightly lit show.
Kewpie dolls, amid such happy tunes,
   Hang where they glitter and glow.

There's a merry-go-round, a loop-the-loop,
   There are joyrides and gay slides, too.
Yes, there's a tall giraffe and a teddy bear,
   Stuffed animals like a make-believe zoo.

There are games of skill to try if you will,
   While barkers yell, "Right this way,"
Such prizes to win, big tops to spin,
   The carnival is lit up most gay.

There are balls to throw for dolls that glow;
   There are coins to toss for the win.
Balloons to pop, toy guns to shoot,
   As magical wheels whir and spin.

Gay little booths filled with goodies to eat,
   So many wait there for a treat.
Candy cotton on sticks, ice-cream cones to lick,
   All there on display so neat.

There are big Indian rugs, and painted jugs;
   There are vases and laces of charm.
From Germany, France, Spain, an import chain,
   Have come wares, your heart to warm.

The people roam here, over there, and about;
   Excitement and fervor run high.
Amid noises of shouting and hustling about,
   A ferris wheel turns in the sky.

Now, the carnival's fun for just everyone,
   With colors most bright to see.
Join the crowds gay, just go there today,
   Where laughter and joy run free.

Evelyn V. Bingham

That Old Swimming Hole

A dip in the old swimming hole, what fun
On a hot summer day in June!
While along the bank lay scattered old clothes,
And where nearby the wild flowers bloomed.

The path through the field to that favorite spot
Was trampled all summer till fall;
Now beside that dear path the weeds grow high,
As high as we once were tall.

The stream that flowed into that old swimming hole
Wound through many an old farmer's field,
While along its banks cattle lazily grazed
On just what to them appealed.

Disturbed not were they by laughter and shout
Of children who came each day
To splash or jump from the "big" diving board,
Or simply to float or to wade.

The old swimming hole, just a stone's throw in width,
And the plank diving board still remain;
But neither the cattle which lazily grazed,
Nor the children are seen, who once came.

For the years of our childhood, so joyous,
Have on to eternity rolled;
But it's good to know children still trod the path
To the joys of that old swimming hole.

Lois Pinkerton Fritz

Summertime Fun

Down the trampled little path
When the days were, oh, so hot,
Secluded by trees near a rocky creek
Lay our favorite summer spot.

As you approach this haven
You'll see many a fishin' pole;
You'll hear the shouts and laughter
Coming from the old swimmin' hole.

As soon as all our chores were done,
Under the hot summer sun,
Off we'd dash to the old swimmin' hole
To have ourselves some fun.

There's never been a joy since then
That can even begin to compare
With the fun we had at the swimmin' hole
As we dived and shouted there.

Ruth H. Underhill

The Old Front Porch

When spring blossomed into summer
And days grew long and hot,
The old front porch and wicker chairs
Became the gathering spot
Of neighbors and friends who came to call
And sit in the soothing shade,
To talk over what was happening
And sip cool lemonade.

And as the shadows lengthened,
The crickets came about,
And evening sounds then took the place
Of the children's playful shouts.

Friends drifted away till dinner was done,
Then often again returned
To while away more hours
As the lamplights softly burned.
A summertime enjoyment,
That ended when fall would appear . . .
A treasure of fond memory
To store for a future year.

Shirley Sallay

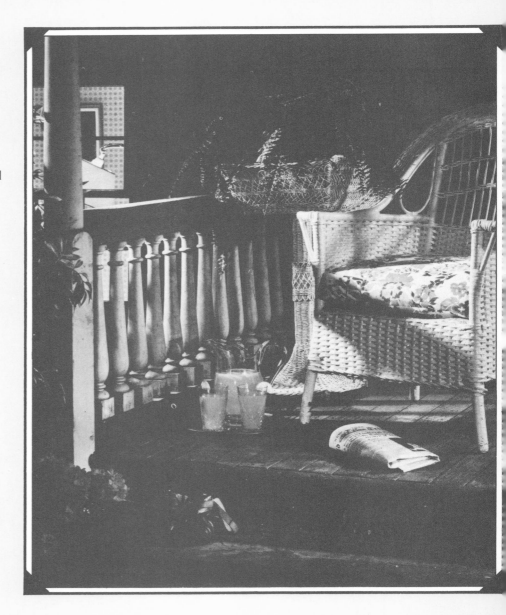

Summertime

Summertime, oh summertime,
What memories lie there.
Summertime, lovely summertime,
With memories to share.

Meadows of green, the clover's scent,
Lazy days, idly spent,
The fishing hole, the willow tree,
The happy spot meant just for me,
Long, long walks in the shady wood . . .
Relive those days, I wish I could.

Yes, I recall those summer days . . .
The rising sun, the morning haze,
Warm evenings spent on the old porch swing,
Ah, there's so much to enjoy
When you're remembering.

Nicole Myers

The Old Porch Swing

Well I remember the old porch swing
Where I could dream away,
Or sip a frosty lemonade
On a lazy summer day.

There Susie entertained her beau
Or Mama sat to mend;
There I often went to read
Or pass time with a friend.

I loved the lulling motion
As back and forth I'd sway,
To watch the twinkling stars at night
Or the rambling rose by day.

Now the old porch swing is obsolete
But the memories linger near,
And I sometimes wish I could return
To the porch swing of yesteryear.

Becky Jennings

Then the delight of "picking" the wild berries! It is one of the fragrant memories of boyhood. Indeed, for boy or man to go a-berrying in a certain pastoral country I know of, where a passer-by along the highway is often regaled by a breeze loaded with a perfume of the o'erripe fruit, is to get nearer to June than by almost any course I know of. . . .

John Burroughs

I n one place we noticed several deep parallel grooves, made by the old glaciers. In the depressions on the summit there was a hard, black, peaty-like soil that looked indescribably ancient and unfamiliar. Out of this mold, which might have come from the moon or the interplanetary spaces, were growing mountain cranberries and blueberries or huckleberries. We were soon so absorbed in gathering the latter that we were quite oblivious of the grandeurs about us.

John Burroughs

Berry-picking Time

It's berry-picking time once more.
　They're up at break of day
To gather all their pans and pails
　And hurry on their way,

With sandwiches stored in a box,
　A jug of lemonade,
Some tasty fruit stored in a sack,
　Some cookies Mother made.

Sunbonnets on the little girls,
　Straw hats on all the boys,
They're off on berry-picking day
　To grasp its wholesome joys.

They comb the banks beside the stream
　Where berries can be found.
They never drop a single one,
　Unheeded, on the ground.

And when the sun shines hot and bright
　From midday's azure dome,
They sit and eat and rest a bit
　Before they start for home.

And when at last they view their hoard,
　As pirates view their gold,
Their minds are filled with treats they'll have
　In spite of snow and cold . . .

All kinds of jam and juice and jell
　And pies with golden crusts;
A bit of summertime to warm
　The winter's icy gusts.

Josephine Millard

65

> *But the favorite haunt of the wild straw-berry is an uplying meadow that has been exempt from the plow for five or six years and that has little timothy and much daisy. . . .*
>
> John Burroughs

The strawberry is always the hope of the invalid and sometime, no doubt, his salvation. It is the first and finest relish among fruits, and well merits Dr. Boteler's memorable saying, that "doubtless God could have made a better berry, but doubtless God never did."

On the threshold of summer, nature proffers us this her virgin fruit; more rich and sumptuous are to follow, but the wild delicacy and fillip of the strawberry are never repeated—that keen feathered edge greets the tongue in nothing else.

Let me not be afraid of overpraising it, but probe and probe for words to hint its surprising virtues. We may well celebrate it with festivals and music. It has that indescribable quality of all first things—that shy, uncloying, provoking barbed sweetness. It is eager and sanguine as youth. It is born of the copious dews, the fragrant nights, the tender skies, the plentiful rains of the early season. The singing of birds is in it, and the health and frolic of lusty nature. It is the product of liquid May touched by the June sun. It has the tartness, the briskness, the unruliness of spring, and the aroma and intensity of summer.

Oh the strawberry days! how vividly they come back to one! The smell of clover in the fields, of blooming rye on the hills, of the wild grape beside the woods, and of the sweet honeysuckle and spiraea about the house. The first hot, moist days. The daisies and buttercups; the songs of the birds, their first reckless jollity and love-making over; the full tender foliage of the trees; the bees swarming and the air strung with resonant musical chords. The time of the sweetest and most succulent grass,

when the cows come home with aching udders. Indeed, the strawberry belongs to the juiciest time of the year.

What a challenge it is to the taste! how it bites back again! and is there any other sound like the snap and crackle with which it salutes the ear on being plucked from the stem? It is a threat to one sense that the other is soon to

verify. It snaps to the ear as it smacks to the tongue. All other berries are tame beside it.

John Burroughs

On this hot and humid day we have the feeling we are seeing fungi at their best. Rising from the damp woodland mold, clus-tered on decaying stumps, growing on the bark of dying trees, dense on moldering logs—some like parasols, some like clubs, some like shelves, some like dense hair, some like masses of coral—fungi, in their varied forms and sizes and colors, arrest our attention all along the way.

Edwin Way Teale

As I was going up the hill, I was surprised to see rising above the June grass, near a walnut, a whitish object, like a stone with a white top, or a skunk erect, for it was black below. It was an enormous toadstool, or fungus, a sharply conical parasol in the form of a sugar loaf, slightly turned up at the edges, which were rent half an inch for every inch or two. . . . It was so delicate and fragile that its whole cap trembled at the least touch, and as I could not lay it down without injuring it, I was obliged to carry it home all the way in my hand, erect, while I paddled my boat with one hand. It was a wonder how its soft cone ever broke through the earth.

Henry David Thoreau

August, too, is the month of the mushrooms—those curious abnormal flowers of a hidden or subterranean vegetation, invoked by heat and moisture from darkness and decay as the summer wanes. Do they not suggest something sickly and uncanny in Nature? Her unwholesome dreams and night fancies, her pale superstitions; her myths and legends and occult lore taking shape in them, spectral and fantastic, at times hinting something libidinous and unseemly: vegetables with gills, fiberless, bloodless; earth-flesh, often offensive, unclean, immodest, often of rare beauty and delicacy, of many shades and colors—creamy white, red, yellow, brown—now the hue of an orange, now of a tomato, now of a potato, some edible, some poisonous, some shaped like spread umbrellas, some like umbrellas reversed by the wind—the sickly whims and fancies of Nature, some imp of the earth mocking and travestying the things of the day. Under my evergreens I saw a large white disk struggling up through the leaves and the debris like the full moon through clouds and vapors.

John Burroughs

In nature the shades of green are infinitely varied. But one of the most beautiful of all is the dark, rich green of a healthy cornfield. . . .

Edwin Way Teale

. . . none of the scenes that returned before our inward eye brought more delight than the remembrance of green corn, row on row, with banner leaves all flowing in the wind. This greater grass, the corn or maize, has a fluid, graceful, impressive beauty of its own.

Edwin Way Teale

One stalk of corn, on a summer day, will raise and disperse into the air as much as a gallon of water. During its growing season, an acre of corn may evaporate into the air above it 300,000 gallons. It has been calculated that if all the water expelled by the leaves of the corn were collected into a lake, it would stand five feet deep across the length and breadth of the cornfield.

Edwin Way Teale

A spectacular feature of all these tall stalks that filled the landscape was the swiftness of their growth. The stems of most plants ascended through the multiplication and expansion of cells at their upper tips. They have a single point of growth. Corn, on the other hand, may have many points of growth. When it is young, it has growing centers not only at its upper tip but between each pair of joints on the lower stalk. It stretches out like the sliding legs of a tripod. It may develop from a kernel to a stalk twenty feet high between spring and September. In eight weeks, it may grow from a seed to a plant with 1,400 square inches of leaf surface. Its combined root system may total seven miles. . . .

Edway Way Teale

Corn

Come walk with me the fields in May
And give this adage heed:
When oak leaves are a mouse's ear
The soil awaits the seed.

The sky is blue, the air is mild,
The soil rolls from one's hand.
The harrowed earth is pillow soft—
It's time to plant the land.

The kernels sprout, the corn will grow,
Be "knee-high by the Fourth"—
As day by day the summer sun
Climbs ever farther north.

And shoulder-high by mid-July
Will grow the stalwart corn
Through tasseling stage, through silking stage—
And, lo, an ear is born.

The milk stage finds the kernel soft;
The dent stage makes advance.
And when the husk is brown and dry,
It's harvest by a glance.

From kernel to an ear of corn,
The cycle is complete—
And he who plants and he who picks
Shall have new corn to eat.

Minnie Klemme

> *What a wonderful thing is the grass, so common, so abundant, so various, a green summer snow that softens the outlines of the landscape, that makes a carpet for the foot, that brings a hush to the fields, and that furnishes food to so many and such various creatures! More than the grazing animals live upon the grass. All our cereals—wheat, barley, rye, rice, oats, corn—belong to the great family of the grasses.*
>
> *John Burroughs*

Standing on J. P. Brown's land, south side, I observed his rich and luxuriant uncut grasslands northward, now waving under the easterly wind. It is a beautiful camilla, sweeping like waves of light and shade over the whole breadth of his land, like a low steam curling over it, imparting wonderful life to the landscape, like the light and shade of a changeable garment, . . . like waves hastening to break on a shore. It is an interesting feature, very easily overlooked, and suggests that we are wading and navigating at present in a sort of sea of grass, which yields and undulates under the wind like water; and so, perchance, the forest is seen to do from a favorable position. Early, there was that flashing light of waving pine in the horizon; now, the Camilla on grass and grain.

The meadow presents a pleasing picture before it is invaded by the haymakers, and a varied and animated one after it is thus invaded; the mowing machine sending a shudder ahead of it through the grass, the hay tedder kicking up the green locks like a giant, many-legged grasshopper, the horse rake gathering the cured hay into windrows, the white-sleeved men with their forks pitching it into cocks, and lastly the huge, soft-cheeked loads of hay, towering above the teams that draw them, brushing against the barways and the lower branches of the trees along their course, slowly winding their way toward the barn. Then the great mows of hay, or the shapely stacks in the fields, and the battle is won. Milk and cream are stored up in well-cured hay, and when the snow of winter fills

Henry David Thoreau

the meadows as grass fills them in summer, the tranquil cow can still rest and ruminate in contentment.

John Burroughs

Somewhere along our way, on some nameless country road, we passed a hayfield at sunset. The windrows curved away like brown rollers in a surf of sun-dried grass, each shot through with shadings of tan and gold and yellow-green. Redwings rode on the crests of these windrow-waves while grackles, hunting crickets and grasshoppers, investigated caverns in the hay. The air, resting at the end of the day, lay calm, redolent with the early summer perfume of the drying grass.

Edwin Way Teale

This is food for man. The earth labors not in vain; it is bearing its burden. The yellow, waving, rustling rye extends far up and over the hills on either side, a kind of pinafore to nature, leaving only a narrow and dark passage at the bottom of a deep ravine. How rankly it has grown! How it hastes to maturity! I discover that there is such a goddess as Ceres. These long grainfields which you must respect, —must go round,—occupying the ground like an army. The small trees and shrubs seen dimly in its midst are overwhelmed by the grain as by an inundation. They are seen only as indistinct forms of bushes and green leaves mixed with the yellow stalks. There are certain crops which give me the idea of bounty, of the *Alma Natura*. They are the grains. Potatoes do not so fill the lap of earth. This rye excludes everything else and takes possession of the soil. The farmer says, "Next year I will raise a crop of rye;" and he proceeds to clear away the brush, and either plows it, or, if it is too uneven or stony, burns and harrows it only, and scatters the seed with faith. And all winter the earth keeps his secret, —unless it did leak out somewhat in the fall,— and in the spring this early green on the hillsides betrays him. When I see this luxuriant crop spreading far and wide in spite of rock and bushes and unevenness of ground, I cannot help thinking that it must have been unexpected by the farmer himself, and regarded by him as a lucky accident for which to thank fortune. This, to reward a transient faith, the gods had given. As if he must have forgotten that he did it, until he saw the waving grain inviting his sickle.

Henry David Thoreau

Out in the Fields with God

The little cares that fretted me
    I lost them yesterday
Among the fields, above the sea,
    Among the winds at play,
Among the lowing of the herds,
    The rustling of the trees,
Among the singing of the birds,
    The humming of the bees.

The foolish fears of what might happen,
    I cast them all away,
Among the clover-scented grass,
    Among the new mown hay,
Among the husking of the corn,
    Where drowsy poppies nod,
Where ill thoughts die and good are born—
    Out in the fields with God.

Author Unknown

71

How well-behaved are cows! When they approach me reclining in the shade, from curiosity, or to receive a whisp of grass, or to share the shade, or to lick the dog held up like a calf—though just now they ran at him to toss him—they do not obtrude. Their company is acceptable, for they can endure the longest pause; they have not got to be entertained. They occupy the most eligible lots in the town. I love to see some pure white about them; they suggest the more neatness.

Henry David Thoreau

Indeed, all the ways and doings of cattle are pleasant to look upon, whether grazing in the pasture, or browsing in the woods, or ruminating under the trees, or feeding in the stall, or reposing upon the knolls. There is virtue in the cow; she is full of goodness; a wholesome odor exhales from her; the whole landscape looks out of her soft eyes; the quality and the aroma of miles of meadow and pasture lands are in her presence and products. I had rather have the care of cattle than be the keeper of the great seal of the nation. Where the cow is, there is Arcadia; so far as her influence prevails, there is contentment, humility, and sweet, homely life.

John Burroughs

I wonder that Wilson Flagg did not include the cow among his "Picturesque Animals," for that is where she belongs. She has not the classic beauty of the horse, but in picture-making qualities she is far ahead of him. Her shaggy, loose-jointed body; her irregular, sketchy outlines, like those of the landscape—the hollows and ridges, the slopes and prominences; her tossing horns, her bushy tail, her swinging gait, her tranquil, ruminating habits —all tend to make her an object upon which the artist eye loves to dwell. The artists are forever putting her into pictures, too. In rural landscape scenes she is an important feature. Behold her grazing in the pastures and on the hillsides, or along banks of streams, or ruminating under wide-spreading trees, or standing belly-deep in the creek or pond, or lying upon the smooth places in the quiet summer afternoon, the day's grazing done, and waiting to be summoned home to be milked; and again in the twilight lying upon the level summit of the hill, or where the sward is thickest and softest; or in winter a herd of them filing along toward the spring to drink, or being "foddered" from the stack in the field upon the new snow—surely the cow is a picturesque animal, and all her goings and comings are pleasant to behold.

John Burroughs

The cow has at least four tones or lows. First, there is her alarmed or distressed low when deprived of her calf, or separated from her mates—her low of affection. Then there is her call of hunger, a petition for food, sometimes full of impatience, or her answer to the farmer's call, full of eagerness. Then there is that peculiar frenzied bawl she utters on smelling blood, which causes every member of the herd to lift its head and hasten to the spot—

What a variety of individualities a herd of cows presents when you have come to know them all, not only in form and color, but in manners and disposition!

John Burroughs

the native cry of the clan. When she is gored or in great danger she bawls also, but that is different. And lastly, there is the long, sonorous volley she lets off on the hills or in the yard, or along the highway, and which seems to be expressive of a kind of unrest and vague longing—the longing of the imprisoned Io for her lost identity. She sends her voice forth so that every god on Mount Olympus can hear her plaint. She makes this sound in the morning, especially in the spring, as she goes forth to graze.

John Burroughs

What a variety of individualities a herd of cows presents when you have come to know them all, not only in form and color, but in manners and disposition! Some are timid and awkward, and the butt of the whole herd. Some remind you of deer. Some have an expression in the face like certain persons you have known. A petted and well-fed cow has a benevolent and gracious look; an ill-used and poorly fed one, a pitiful and forlorn look. Some cows have a masculine or ox expression; others are extremely feminine. The latter are the ones for milk. Some cows will kick like a horse; some jump fences like deer. Every herd has its ringleader, its unruly spirit—one that plans all the mischief and leads the rest through the fences into the grain or into the orchard. This one is usually quite different from the master spirit, the "boss of the yard." The latter is generally the most peaceful and law-abiding cow in the lot, and the least bullying and quarrelsome. But she is not to be trifled with; her will is law; the whole herd give way before her, those that have crossed horns with her and those that have not, but yielded their allegiance without crossing. . . .

John Burroughs

Haying Time

I like to see the country folk
Go haying in the field;
There is a peace, a deep concern,
For what their pastures yield.

I like to smell the fragrance,
The sweetness of the hay,
That perfumes all the countryside
Upon a summer's day.

I like to see it cut and tied
With labor and with pride,

Then taken to the barn and stacked
For wintertime, inside.

I like to see the country folk
When haying time is done,
Gather round the country store
To talk, relax with fun.

I like to hear them brag and boast
That their crop was the best,
And now that haying time was o'er,
They'd settle down to rest.

Gertrude Rudberg

Many cattle need much hay; hence in dairy sections haying is the period of "storm and stress" in the farmer's year. To get the hay in, in good condition, and before the grass gets too ripe, is a great matter. All the energies and resources of the farm are bent to this purpose. It is a thirty or forty-day war, in which the farmer and his "hands" are pitted against the heat and the rain and the legions of timothy and clover. Everything about it has the urge, the hurry, the excitement of a battle. Outside help is procured; men flock in from adjoining counties, where the ruling industry is something else and is less imperative; coopers, blacksmiths, and laborers of various kinds drop their tools, and take down their scythes and go

"pointing out" is perfect, and you can hardly see the ribs of his swath. He stands up to his grass and strikes level and sure. He will turn a double down through the stoutest grass, and when the hay is raked away you will not find a spear left standing.

John Burroughs

Many of our old neighbors toiled and sweated and grubbed themselves into their graves years before their natural dying days, in getting a living on a quarter-section of land and vaguely trying to get rich, while bread and raiment might have been serenely won on less than a fourth of this land, and time gained to get better acquainted with God.

In those early days, long before the great labor-saving machines came to our help, almost everything connected with wheat-raising abounded in trying work—cradling in the long, sweaty dog-days, raking and binding, stacking, thrashing—and it often seemed to me that our fierce, over-industrious way of getting the grain from the ground was too closely connected with grave-digging. The staff of life, naturally beautiful, oftentimes suggested the grave-digger's spade. Men and boys, and in those days even women and girls, were cut down while cutting the wheat. The fat folk grew lean and the lean leaner, while the rosy cheeks brought from Scotland and other cool countries across the sea faded to yellow like the wheat. We were all made slaves through the vice of over-industry. The same was in great part true in making hay to keep the cattle and horses through the long winters. We were called in the morning at four o'clock and seldom got to bed before nine, making a broiling, seething day seventeen hours long loaded with heavy work, while I was only a small stunted boy; . . .

John Muir

The Wagon

I can hear them today. I can hear those
    old wheels
As they rattle and clatter along,
For the sound faintly drifts through
    the many long years
Like the tune of an old-fashioned song.

I can smell the sweet fragrance
    of alfalfa hay
Piled high on the stout wagon bed,
And I sit like a monarch upon that
    great throne
While the sunshine is warm on my head.

I still sway with the motion of wagon
    and hay,
And the rhythm brings rapture untold,
And I know the sweet dreams that I dreamed
    on that throne
In those wonderful days long ago.

Now my thoughts often drift to the long,
    long ago
And that wagon of sweet-scented hay,
And I grasp just a bit of that fragrance
    and peace
That is wafted from yesterday.

Josephine Millard

Hay-gathering is clean, manly work all through. Young fellows work in haying who do not do another stroke on the farm the whole year. It is a gymnasium in the meadows and under the summer sky. How full of pictures, too—the smooth slopes dotted with cocks with lengthening shadows; the great, broad-backed, soft-cheeked loads, moving along the lanes and brushing under the trees; the unfinished stack with forkfuls of hay being

in quest of a job in haying. Every man is expected to pitch his endeavors in a little higher key than at any other kind of work. The wages are extra, and the work must correspond. The men are in the meadow by half-past four or five in the morning, and mow an hour or two before breakfast. A good mower is proud of his skill. He does not "lop in," and his

The Harvest

Reapers have been busy with
The harvesting of fields
Which have responded to earth's call
With rich abundant yields.

The sickles clicking merrily
Seem pleased with nature's plan
Of planting, growth and harvesting
The food required by man.

Thick upon the stubbled land,
The shocks of ripened grain
Are springtime's promises fulfilled
By summer's sun and rain.

To grace this cornucopia
Of nature's treasure trove,
The August moon spreads eerie charm
On fruited field and grove.

Clara B. Dice Roe

I am glad to observe that all the poetry of the midsummer harvesting has not gone out with the scythe and the whetstone. The line of mowers was a pretty sight, if one did not sympathize too deeply with the human backs turned up there to the sun, and the sound of the whetstone, coming up from the meadows in the dewy morning, was pleasant music. But I find the sound of the mowing machine and the patent reaper are even more in tune with the voices of Nature at this season. The characteristic sounds of midsummer are the sharp, whirring crescendo of the cicada or harvest fly, and the rasping, stridulous notes of the nocturnal insects. The mowing machine repeats and imitates these sounds. 'Tis like the hum of a locust or the shuffling of a mighty grasshopper. More than that, the grass and the grain at this season have become hard. The timothy stalk is like a file; the rye straw is glazed with flint; the grasshoppers snap sharply as they fly up in front of you; the birdsongs have ceased; the ground crackles underfoot; the eye of day is brassy and merciless; and in harmony with all these things is the rattle of the mower and hay-tedder.

John Burroughs

handed up its sides to the builder, and when finished the shape of a great pear, with a pole in the top for the stem.

John Burroughs

Machinery, I say, has taken away some of the picturesque features of farm life. How much soever we may admire machinery and the faculty of mechanical invention, there is no machine like a man; and the work done directly by his hands, the things made or fashioned by them, have a virtue and a quality that cannot be imparted by machinery. The line of mowers in the meadows, with the straight swaths behind them, are more picturesque than the "Clipper" or "Buckeye" mower, with its team and driver. So are the flails of the threshers, chasing each other through the air, more pleasing to the eye and the ear than the machine, with its uproar, its choking clouds of dust, and its general hurly-burly.

John Burroughs

Certainly a midsummer day in the country, with all its sights and sounds, its singing birds, its skimming swallows, its grazing or ruminating cattle, its drifting cloud shadows, its grassy perfumes from the meadows and the hillsides, and the farmer with his men and teams busy with the harvest, has material for the literary artist. A good hay day is a good day for the writer and the poet, because it has a certain crispness and pureness; it is positive; it is rich in sunshine; there is a potency in the blue sky which you feel; the high barometer raises your spirits; your thoughts ripen as the hay cures. You can sit in a circle of shade beneath a tree in the fields or in front of the open hay-barn doors, as I do, and feel the fruition and satisfaction of nature all about you. The brimming meadows seem fairly to purr as the breezes stroke them; the trees rustle their myriad leaves as if in gladness; the many-colored butterflies dance by; the steel blue of the swallows' backs glistens in the sun as they

The Threshing Machine

When summer has ended and all down the lane
The wheat fields are waving with ripe golden grain,
When orchards are heavy with fruit on the bough
And barns are o'erflowing with hay in the mow,
Then I love to remember the wonderful scene
That was made by the old-fashioned threshing machine.

Wood fed to the boiler turned water to steam
And pulling the throttle, the whistle would scream.
With a chug and a hiss and belching black smoke
The belt whirred and flapped as the engine was stoked.
Through a galvanized pipe the straw blew to a stack,
And the clean golden grain streamed into a sack.

The farmers all gathered with banter and laughs,
Their faces suntanned and dusted with chaff.
A long train of teams came in from the fields,
Drawing the wagons with summer's rich yield.
From sheaves of full grain that the binder had reaped
The bins were soon filled with bright golden heaps.

We children stood round, all watching with awe
The mightiest engine that ever we saw.
The shiny tin bucket with water we filled,
And drank from the dipper with many a spill.
The small boys longed for the day when they, too,
Would be able to work with the big threshing crew.

The big kitchen buzzed with gay womenfolk
As they hustled and bustled with laughter and jokes.
The range was all covered with kettles and pans.
No one ever tasted a dinner so grand.
They washed in a basin set out on the porch
Then to the long table the hungry crew marched.

Our modern-day combines, efficient and new,
Do more in a day than a twelve-man crew.
But I love to recall the neighborly scene
That was made by the old-fashioned threshing machine.

Marion Olson

skim the fields, and the mellow boom of the passing bumblebee but enhances the sense of repose and contentment that pervades the air. The hay cures; the oats and corn deepen their hue; the delicious fragrance of the last wild strawberries is on the breeze; your mental skies are lucid, and life has the midsummer fullness and charm.

A high barometer is best for the haymakers and it is best for the human spirits. When the smoke goes straight up, one's thoughts are more likely to soar also and revel in the higher air. The persons who do not like to get up in the morning till the day has been well sunned and aired evidently thrive best on a high barometer. Such days do seem better ventilated, and our lungs take in fuller draughts of air. How curious it is that the air should seem heavy to us when it is light, and light when it is heavy! On those sultry, muggy days when it is an effort to move and the grasshopper is a burden, the air is light, and we are in the trough of the vast atmospheric wave; while we are on its crest and are buoyed up both in mind and in body, on the crisp, bright days when the air seems to offer us no resistance. We know that the heavier salt sea water buoys us up more than the fresh river or pond water, but we do not feel in the same way the lift of the high barometric wave.

John Burroughs

Last Days of Summer

I love a warm earth-scented day
  That smells of clover and new hay,
Wild mint and meadow rue and pine . . .
  When open blooms of columbine
Spill fragrance with an open hand
  Upon a clean and sober land.

A day that from the sunrise on
  Fulfills the promise of the dawn,
Steeped in the odors of the field
  Where apple orchards faintly yield
The essence of the bark and root
  And the warm odor of the fruit . . .

When waves of perfume lifting high
  Ascend the ladders of the sky,
Like incense in a cloistered church;
  When little clumps of growing birch
Unlock their treasure troves and spill
  Their fragrance over dale and hill.

A day when summer's at its peak
  And all creation seems to speak
A lovely language of its own,
  When warm earth-scented winds are blown
Across the fields where flowers white
  Look like small faces in the night.

I almost feel at times like these
That I could worship fields and trees.

Edna Jaques

August, the aureate month, draws to its blazing close—a month of sun, if ever there was one. Gold in the grain on the round-backed hill fields. Gold in the wood sunflowers, and in the summer goldenrod waving plumes all through the woodlot, trooping down the meadow to the brookside, marching in the dust of the roadways. Gold in the wing of the wild canaries, dipping and twittering as they flit from weed to bush, as if invisible waves of air tossed them up and down. The orange and yellow clover butterflies seek out the thistle, and the giant sulphur swallowtails are in their final brood. The amber, chaff-filled dust gilds all the splendid sunsets in cloudless, burning skies. Long, long after the sun has set, the sun-drenched earth gives back its heat, radiates it to the dim stars; the moon gets up in gold; before it lifts behind the black fields to the east I take it for a rick fire, till it rises like an old gold coin, that thieves have clipped on one worn edge.

Donald Culross Peattie

August days are for the most part tranquil days; the fret and hurry of the season are over. We are on the threshold of autumn. Nature dreams and meditates; her veins no longer thrill with the eager, frenzied sap; she ripens and hardens her growths; she concentrates; she begins to make ready for winter. The buds for next year are formed during this month and her nuts and seeds and bulbs finish storing up food for the future plant.

John Burroughs

I mark the summer's swift decline,
The springing sward its grave clothes weaves
Whose rustling woods the gales confine,
The aged year turns on its couch of leaves.

Oh, could I catch the sounds remote,
Could I but tell to human ear
The strains which on the breezes float
And sing the requiem of the dying year.

Henry David Thoreau

Golden Hours of Summer

Where summer basks neath peaceful skies
The spell of perfect weather lies,
Bright meadow flowers congregate
Where raucous starlings hold debate,
And sheep in pastures graze serene
Beside stone walls where bluejays preen.
The children spend each sunny day
In games that small fry love to play.

The bright days stretch in lazy ease
Beneath the shade of willow trees,
Where busy insects toil to hoard
The winter fare lush fields afford.
They have no time for pleasure's lure;
They first must winter's stores assure,
But elsewhere in the world of sun
The main concern is having fun.

Summer lives briefly, rich and well,
To lavish charm in vale and dell.
She's not concerned with somber way
She lives to savor carefree days.
Her flowered mantle spreads the scen
Of perfumed days in gladness spent.
She brings the land the gentle spell
Of golden hours when all is well.

Brian F. King